Transition and Transformation
Fostering Transfer Student Success

Transition and Transformation
Fostering Transfer Student Success

Stephen J. Handel & Eileen Strempel

Dahlonega, GA

Project Editor:
Judith T. Brauer

Published by:
University of North Georgia Press
Dahlonega, Georgia

Printing Support by:
Booklogix Publishing Services, Inc
Alpharetta, Georgia

Cover and book design by Corey Parson

ISBN: 978-1-940771-25-0

Printed in the United States of America, 2016
For more information, please visit ung.edu/university-press
Or email ungpress@ung.edu

CONTENTS

EPILOGUE   135

Eileen Strempel

About **NISTS**

The National Institute for the Study of Transfer Students (NISTS) exists to improve the lives of transfer students. Through research, education, and service, we support professionals who directly serve transfer students, as well as those who create transfer policy and conduct transfer-related research. NISTS bridges knowledge, policies, and practice by bringing together a wide range of stakeholders to explore the issues related to the transfer process in order to facilitate student success and degree completion. We partner with two- and four-year institutions, state agencies, higher education associations, foundations, and others committed to transfer student success.

NISTS was founded in 2002 by Dr. Bonita C. Jacobs in response to a lack of professional development opportunities and research literature focused specifically on transfer students. Since that time, NISTS has contributed to the national conversation about transfer students in many ways. NISTS has been awarded multiple grants to conduct transfer-related research and to host symposiums to disseminate the findings. In addition, NISTS advisory board members and staff have produced authoritative transfer-related publications, resources, and presentations. This peer-reviewed monograph is part of an annual series published by the National Institute for the Study of Transfer Students designed to highlight and share promising practices in supporting transfer students.

NISTS held its inaugural conference at the University of North Texas with 300 attendees from over thirty higher education institutions and thirty-two states. More than ten years later, the fourteenth annual conference brings together nearly 500 attendees from thirty-seven states and two provinces in Canada. The NISTS conference is the only annual gathering of its kind, specifically focused on transfer. It is unique in bringing together a wide range of professionals from across functional areas, institutional types, systems, and sectors to comprehensively focus on transfer research, policy, and practice.

NISTS continues to encourage transfer-related research and best practices in a variety of ways. In 2006, NISTS began offering grants to support transfer-related research, and in 2010 we introduced and awarded the first Barbara K. Townsend Dissertation of the Year Award. In 2013, we introduced an opportunity to recognize outstanding transfer professionals with the inaugural Bonita C. Jacobs Transfer Champions Award. And in 2014, we expanded this award to also recognize Rising Stars, those with a shorter tenure, but whose impact is significant.

NISTS also offers exclusive access to members-only resources, including institute research and conference proceedings as well as related policy information, a newsletter, discounts for NISTS professional development events, and more through our membership organization, the Association for the Study of Transfer Students (ASTS).

Learn more about NISTS and join ASTS by visiting: transferinstitute.org .

PREFACE

Stephen J. Handel

TRANSFER NATION

In a country devoted to the idea of education as a means of economic and social ascent—a land of opportunity where one is theoretically limited only by the extent and quality of effort—the transfer process remains one of the most imaginative yet least understood initiatives in higher education. As the central mission of community colleges—a uniquely American creation—the transfer process remains the audacious conceit of visionary education leaders who believed that the US would profit economically and culturally by creating a new avenue to the four-year degree. Under this scheme, individuals hampered by socioeconomic or geographic limitation could attend an open access community college and prepare themselves for transfer to a four-year institution in virtually any major field. From its earliest beginnings, the possibility of the transfer process has turned the notion of elite education on its head by demonstrating that almost anyone with ambition and drive could scale the academic heights previously only experienced by the most privileged.

As American higher education grew in the twentieth century, so did the community college sector and the transfer process. Today nearly half of all undergraduates in America begin postsecondary education at a two-year college, over seven million students at 1,123 institutions (American Association of Community Colleges, 2015). Yet transfer, for all of its progressive intentions, languished in the latter part of the last century and has yet to gain significant traction in the first decade of the new one (Handel & Williams, 2012). While most first-time community college students express an intent to transfer and earn the baccalaureate degree, only a small proportion succeed in doing so (Bailey, Jaggars, & Jensen, 2015). We believe that this disconnect has more to do with institutional provincialism rather than an explicit hostility to transfer. A narrow focus on institution-specific goals can discourage a broader conversation on addressing the needs of community college students who have the tenacity and skill to earn a baccalaureate degree.

Fortunately, a decade and a half into this new century, there is a robust debate concerning the nation's higher education priorities, a byproduct of the Great Recession's reordering of the financial landscape for many American families (see Carey, 2015; Mettler, 2014; Zakaria, 2015). Although the rhetoric is sometimes focused on relatively limited concerns around workforce needs and the economic payoff of a college education, the discussion holds promise for a reinvigorated transfer process, as illustrated in the pages of this monograph. The pervasive theme is that the potential of the transfer process awaits only the thoughtful implementation of strategies and best practices by staff, faculty and policymakers committed to the fundamental tenets of higher education access and diversity.

A Focus on Completion Rates

Students' completion rates at our nation's colleges and universities have been the subject of extraordinary attention by the current presidential administration and state legislatures around the country (Blumenstyk, 2015; Complete College America, 2014). Unhappy with rising tuition costs, yet convinced of the importance of a college-educated citizenry, lawmakers want colleges and universities to become more efficient while awarding degrees to a broader sector of the American populace. For their part, prospective students and families wish to leverage limited higher education resources in ways that manage college costs, reduce college-related debt, and lead to certificates and degrees that have value in an uncertain marketplace (New, 2015).

Balancing college costs and completion rates, lawmakers and families have increasingly turned their attention to two-year community colleges. The cost calculus is a simple one. Unburdened by traditional overhead at four-year research universities, support of community colleges is a less costly proposition for state governments. Average community college tuition is a fraction of the cost associated with private and public four-year universities. According to the College Board, published tuition costs for in-state students at public community colleges averages $3,347 per year compared to $9,139 at public four-year institutions, and $31,231 at private, not-for-profit institutions (College Board, 2014). Students who spend their first years in a community college completing lower-division, general education coursework may then transfer to a four-year institution to complete the baccalaureate degree. The state saves money by subsidizing students at a lower-cost institution.

For students and families, the selection of a specific college is guided by a variety of factors, including economic gain, employment opportunities, and the chance to learn more about a specific content area or major (Fishman, 2015). Students choosing to attend a community college are also guided by such reasons, but location and cost are especially important. The geographic convenience of community colleges reshaped traditional notions of "going away to college." For example, in places such as California and North Carolina, there is a two-year institution within driving distance of ninety percent of the population. Moreover, students who attend college on a part-time basis while living at home make the economic investment of postsecondary education seem less risky. So, it is not surprising that the community college has become the most popular postsecondary education sector in America (AACC, 2015). Lower-cost and ready-access are an irresistible allure for students from low-income backgrounds. But the attraction for other underrepresented groups of students is equally apparent in a country whose shifting demographics make the term "minority populations" increasingly meaningless. For example, fifty-seven percent of all Hispanic students currently attending postsecondary education are enrolled at a community college, along with fifty-two percent of all African American students and sixty-one percent of Native American students (AACC, 2015). And, contrary to popular stereotypes, Asian American and Pacific Islander students are more likely to enroll at a community college than a selective four-year university (Teranishi, 2008-; Campaign for College Opportunity, 2015).

TRANSFER: WHAT IT IS, WHAT IT PROMISES, AND WHAT IT DELIVERS

Although community colleges are now the most popular choice of American college students, these institutions are only about a century old. Established in earnest at the beginning of the twentieth century, "junior colleges," were a populist outgrowth of a nation hungry for self-improvement and looking for means of economic prosperity (Witt, Wattenbarger, Gollattscheck, & Suppiger, 1994; Brint & Karable, 1989). Championed by leaders at the nation's most prominent four-year institutions such as Stanford, Michigan, and Berkeley, these two-year institutions would serve as a bridge between the traditional high school diploma and the more elite bachelor's degree which, at that time, was earned by an extremely small portion of the U.S. population (Beach, 2011; Dougherty, 1996).

The idea of a transfer pathway is central to the original mission of the community college (Brint & Karabel, 1989). However this founding ideal is sometimes forgotten (Handel 2013a). Today's political rhetoric tends to focus on the need for students to earn a marketable credential or skill, and is often seen as the *only* aim of the community college. Since World War II, when the full flowering of the community college came into being, its leaders have emphasized the creation of "terminal" degrees and credentials (Eells, 1941; Koos, 1925/1970). The federal government has supported this notion by providing resources to establish workforce training programs and vocational studies that prepare students for marketplace skills after one or two years of postsecondary education (Cohen & Brawer, 2007). This emphasis accelerated during the Great Recession. With unemployment rates hovering at historic highs and college completion rates stagnant, the Obama Administration devoted significant support to community colleges to help them rejuvenate an economy in desperate need of a better-educated citizenry (Levin, 2012). Community colleges responded quickly, often more efficiently than their four-year institutional counterparts.

As the nation's economy has strengthened, both state and federal leaders continue to lavish praise on the mission of community colleges for the "practical" and "marketable" thrust of its curricula, as if this sector of higher education alone paved the way for a more competitive America. Make no mistake, associate degrees and certificates are an important part of the postsecondary landscape, even more important now than ever before in a global marketplace increasingly focused on knowledge-based skills (College Board, 2008; Lumina, 2015). However, most students do not view these credentials as "terminal" but rather as a beginning point from which they may springboard to a degree that would allow them to become eligible for graduate school and additional professional training. Research is overwhelming that first-time community college students desire the same outcome that students in elite institutions want: baccalaureate credentials that will help them control their economic future (Bailey, Jaggars, & Jensen, 2015; Handel, 2013b, 2014; Horn, 2009; Horn & Skomsvold, 2011; Provasnik & Planty, 2008).

The data on career earnings justify students' claim on the baccalaureate. Lifetime earnings for an individual with a baccalaureate degree regularly outpace earnings for students with an associate degree or a certificate (Baum, Kurose, & Ma, 2013; Carnevale & Rose, 2011). There are variations, of course. Directly out of college, some associate degree-holders *initially* make more money than individuals with bachelor's degrees. Education pundits and cable news commentators often get a fair bit of mileage out of such studies, condemning four-year colleges for their "worthless" degrees that allegedly trap college graduates as baristas for life. What commentators fail to reveal is that the long-term investment in four-year degrees clearly outpaces outcomes gleaned from degrees and certificates awarded by community colleges. Moreover, the bachelor's degree serves as the credential that prepares students for post-graduate and professional training, where the payoff in career earnings again jumps considerably (Baum, Ma, & Payea, 2013).

THE PIVOTAL ROLE OF FOUR-YEAR INSTITUTIONS

If public four-year institutions are feeling complacent given the degree of interest being shown to the community college, they should reconsider their perspective. The completion rates for these institutions are also under the microscope and the value-for-money calculation—a limiting but powerful metric in the eyes of low- and middle-income Americans—is increasingly seen as risky (Carey, 2015; Crow & Dabars, 2015). How can it be, ask policymakers and families, that the cost of a four-year degree should rise 80 percent in a decade, nearly twice as much as health care (Kurtzleben, 2013; Baum et al., 2014)? Although there are defensible reasons why the cost of a four-year degree should be so expensive—a labor-intensive industry, declining state and federal support, ruinous competition—the sticker shock nonetheless undercuts the mission of these institutions as places where a wide strata of the American populace can attend and earn their place as productive contributors to the economy.

The cost of a college degree has forced lawmakers and others to seek lower-cost solutions. At least part of the rhetoric around the value of a college degree is its power to make up for students' lost opportunity costs while training them to find family-sustaining jobs. However, more thoughtful commentators have identified the moribund transfer process as a potential solution, a solution that satisfies lawmaker's needs for a lower-cost per degree and provides a more affordable avenue to the baccalaureate for cash-strapped families whose sons and daughters might otherwise end up awash in significant college loan debt (Kahlenberg, 2015; Century Foundation, 2013).

Ironically, however, the transfer pathway to the bachelor's degree—for all of its potential advantages in the current economic climate—is not always embraced by the institutions that secure its success: community colleges and four-year institutions (Handel & Williams, 2012). At a recent meeting of the University of California Board of Regents, Governor Jerry Brown recommended that all undergraduates in the state complete their lower-division courses in one of the state's 113 community colleges and then transfer to a campus of the California State University or the University of California (University of California, 2014). Leaders of both four-year systems quietly scoffed at the idea. But Brown's proposal was neither radical nor indecent. He was only echoing the original mission for community colleges. His father, former governor Edmund Brown, was the instigator of Clark Kerr's Master Plan, a proposal intent on making higher education a more egalitarian system primarily through the use of the community college as a springboard to the baccalaureate degree. Yet, as noted earlier, many community college leaders, with some justification, prefer to see their institutions as purveyors of workforce credentials rather than academic farm teams for four-year institutions. Similarly, many university leaders view their institutional mission as molders of youth over four-years rather than two. Indeed, a good deal of the debate around "under-matching"—the often quoted phenomenon in which high-ability, low-income students tend not to apply to colleges that match their academic skills—seems predicated on keeping students *out* of community colleges rather than strengthening the transfer pathway (Bowen, Chingos, & McPherson, 2009; Hoxby & Turner, 2013).

Of course there are many two- and four-year institutions that are actively pursuing the transfer function and many thousands of students who are the direct beneficiaries. But for transfer to meet the potential of its original intent, it must be a more sustained and strategic partnership around the country, born of the same commitment that is currently lavished on first-year students (College Board, 2011). The imbalance of this partnership frequently falls on community colleges, which are held accountable for low transfer rates, even though they represent only one side of the academic equation. Community colleges *prepare* students for the transfer transition, but four-year institutions *admit* students and set the conditions for that admission. Prospective transfer students are often tripped up by conditions of admission that are not well-communicated and the failure of some four-year institutions to accept community college course credit. Unless two- and four-year institutions are authentic partners, transfer students will not be well-served. These students must represent a long-term enrollment commitment on the part of four-year institutions, not merely revenue-generating "back fill" when first-year targets are not met.

The barriers to transfer are well-documented (Beach, 2011; Cohen & Brawer, 2008; Eaton, 1994). Critics highlight curricular misalignment between and among two- and four-year institutions as the core problem. Courses taken at one location may not apply at another (Western Interstate Commission on Higher Education, 2011). But the problem is multifaceted and a variety of strategies are needed. For example, careful planning is key for successful transfer, but the lack of quality, longitudinal advising slows the ability of students to transfer successfully to a four-year institution. It is odd that we ask students with the least knowledge of higher education to plan and implement a convoluted strategy to move from one institution to another in the middle of their academic careers. Such a transition is rarely recommended to students attending four-year institutions and yet those who begin in community colleges must do this as a matter of academic necessity if they wish to earn a bachelor's degree. Lack of sustained guidance combined with the complexity of the transfer process all too frequently places our most vulnerable students at risk of not completing their college degrees.

INNOVATIVE THINKING AROUND TRANSFER

This volume attempts to strengthen the transfer partnership by highlighting the experience of practitioners who are involved in the day-to-day work of serving students in a variety of institutional contexts: public and private, two-year and four-year. The authors hail from institutions around the country, as well as foundations and organizations that are devoted to the important work of improving American higher education. Their insight—often culled from years of experience—provides a set of strategies that will be useful to two- and four-year institution faculty and staff who are interested in improving the transfer process. In addition, this publication will inform policymakers who are grappling with state and national higher education issues and who seek new ideas about closing the achievement gap and increasing higher education completion rates.

The monograph is categorized into three areas: 1) Strategic Planning and Organizational Review; 2) Curricular Innovations; and 3) Outreach and Advising. Each area contains a varied set of chapters that illuminate a particular issue critical for the transfer process.

As detailed above, the transfer function is well positioned to address a number of compelling problems facing higher education in America. Transfer serves families by providing an affordable avenue to higher education while minimizing the impact of crippling loan debt. It serves the public at large by leveraging scarce state resources over the long-term. And it provides a path to higher education for students who might not otherwise have access to it. However, none of these outcomes will be realized unless we improve the transfer process.

The insights and strategies presented in this volume signal an important trend in American higher education. The traditional access mission of community colleges is increasingly being embraced as essential to facilitating baccalaureate degree completion. This can only be accomplished in partnership with four-year institutions, who are equally devoted to access and success for underserved populations. The collective effort of researchers and practitioners described here demonstrates the vital role of the transfer process in advancing the educational dreams of individuals who might not otherwise have access to higher education. It also reveals the breadth and richness of promising strategies designed to prepare students for this life-altering educational journey.

REFERENCES

American Association of Community Colleges. (2015). *Community College Fast Facts*. Retrieved from http://www.aacc.nche.edu/AboutCC/Pages/fastfactsfactsheet.aspx

Baum, S. Kurose, C., & Ma, J. (2013, October). *How College Shapes Lives: Understanding the Issues.* New York: The College Board.

Baum, S., Ma, J., & Payea, K. (2013). *Education Pays: The Benefits of Higher Education for Individuals and Society.* New York: The College Board.

Bailey, T. R., Jaggers S. S., & Jensen, D. (2015). *Redesigning America's community colleges.* Baltimore: The Johns Hopkins Press.

Beach, J. M. (2011). *Gateway to opportunity? A history of the community college in the United States.* Sterling, VA: Stylus Publishing.

Blumentyck, G. (2015). *American higher education in crisis? What everyone needs to know.* New York: Oxford University Press.

Bowen, W. G., Chingos, M. M., & McPherson, M. S. (2009). *Crossing the finish line: Completing college at America's public universities.* Princeton, NJ: Princeton University Press.

Brint, S., & Karabel, J. (1989). *The diverted dream: Community colleges and the promise of educational opportunity in America, 1900–1985.* New York: Oxford University Press.

Campaign for College Opportunity. (2015). *The State of Higher Education in California: Asian American Native Hawaiian Pacific Islander Report. Los Angeles: Campaign for College Opportunity. Retrieved from* http://collegecampaign.org/portfolio/september-2015-the-state-of-higher-education-in-california-asian-american-native-hawaiian-pacific-islander-report/

Carey, K. (2015). *The end of college: Creating the future of learning and the university of everywhere.* New York: Riverhead Books.

Carnevale, A. P., & Rose, S. J. (2011). *The undereducated American.* Retrieved from Georgetown University, Center on Education and the Workforce website: http://cew.georgetown.edu/undereducated

Century Foundation (2013). *Bridging the Higher Education Divide: Strengthening Community Colleges and Restoring the American Dream.* New York: The Century Foundation. Retrieved from http://www.tcf. org/assets/downloads/20130523-Bridging_the_Higher_Education_ Divide-REPORT-ONLY.pdf

Cohen, A. M., & Brawer, F. B. (2008). *The American community college.* San Francisco: Jossey-Bass.

College Board. (2014). *Trends in college pricing 2014.* New York: The College Board. Retrieved from http://trends.collegeboard.org/college-pricing

College Board. (2011). *Improving student transfer from community colleges to four-year institutions — the perspective of leaders from baccalaureate-granting institutions.* New York: The College Board.

College Board. (2008). *Winning The Skills Race And Strengthening The Middle Class: An Action Agenda For Community Colleges.* New York: The College Board. Available at http://professionals.collegeboard.com/ profdownload/winning_the_skills_race.pdf

Complete College America. (2014*). Four-Year Myth: Make College More Affordable. Restore the Promise of Graduating on Time.* Washington DC: Complete College America. Retrieved from http://completecollege.org/wp-content/uploads/2014/11/4-Year-Myth.pdf

Crow, M. M. & Dabars, W. B. (2015). *Designing the new American university.* Baltimore: Johns Hopkins University Press.

Dowd, A. C., Cheslock, J., & Melguizo, T. (2008). Transfer access from community colleges and the distribution of elite higher education. *Journal of Higher Education, 79* (4), 1–31.

Dougherty, K. J. (1994). *The contradictory college: The conflicting origins, impacts, and futures of the community college.* Albany, NY: State University of New York Press.

Eaton, J. S. (1994). *Strengthening collegiate education in community colleges.* San Francisco: Jossey-Bass.

Eells, W. C. (1941). *Present status of junior college terminal education.* Washington, DC: American Association of Junior Colleges.

Fishman, SR. (2015). *Deciding to Go to College: The 2015 College Decisions Survey (Part 1).* Washington DC: New American Foundation. Retrieved from http://dev-edcentral.pantheon.io/wp-content/uploads/2015/05/FINAL-College-Decisions-Survey-528.pdf

Handel, S. J. (2013a). *Recurring Trends and Persistent Themes: A Brief History of Transfer*. New York: The College Board.

Handel, S. J. (2013b). "The Transfer Moment: The Pivotal Partnership Between Community Colleges and Four-Year Institutions in Securing the Nation's College Completion Agenda." In J. L. Marling (Ed.), *Collegiate Transfer: Navigating the New Normal*. (New Directions for Higher Education, No. 162). San Francisco: Jossey-Bass.

Handel S. J. (2014). Community college students earning the baccalaureate degree: The Good news could be better. *College and University Journal*, *89* (No. 2). 22-30.

Handel, S. J. & Williams, R. A. (2012). *The Promise of the Transfer Pathway: Opportunity and Challenge for Community College Students Seeking the Baccalaureate Degree*. New York: The College Board.

Horn, L. (2009). *On track to complete? A taxonomy of beginning community college students and their outcomes 3 years after enrolling: 2003–04 through 2006 (NCES Publication No. 2009-152)*. Washington, DC: National Center for Education Statistics, Institute of Education Sciences, U.S. Department of Education.

Horn, L. & P. Skomsvold. (2011). *Web tables: Community college student outcomes: 1994-2009* (NCES Publication Number 2012-253). Washington DC: National Center for Education Statistics, Institute of Education Sciences, U.S. Department of Education.

Hoxby, C., & Turner, S. (2013). *Expanding college opportunities for high-achieving, low income students*. Stanford Institute for Economic Policy Research. Retrieved from http://siepr.stanford.edu/publicationsprofile/2555

Kahlenberg, R. D. (2015, January 12). The Genius of Obama's Two-year College Proposal. *The Atlantic*. Retrieved from http://www.theatlantic.com/education/archive/2015/01/the-genius-of-obamas-two-year-college-proposal/384429/

Koos, L. V. (1970/1925). *The Junior college movement*. New York: AMS Press

Kurtzleben, D. (2013, October 23). Just how fast has college tuition grown? *US News and World Report*. http://www.usnews.com/news/articles/2013/10/23/charts-just-how-fast-has-college-tuition-grown

Lewin, T. (2012, February 12). Money urged for colleges to perform job training. *The New York Times*.

Lumina Foundation. (2015). *A stronger nation through higher education.* Indianapolis, IN: Lumina Foundation. Retrieved from https://www.luminafoundation.org/stronger_nation

Mettler, S. (2014). *Degrees of inequality: How the politics of higher education sabotaged the American dream.* New York: Basic Books

New, J. (2015, September 29). Not Worth It? *Inside Higher Education.* Retrieved from: https://www.insidehighered.com/news/2015/09/29/half-college-graduates-say-college-worth-cost-survey-finds?utm_source=Inside%20Higher%20Ed&utm_campaign=d5e1f64676-DNU20150929&utm_medium=email&utm_term=0_1fcbc04421-d5e1f64676-198451421

Provasnik, S. & M. Planty (2008). *Community colleges: Special supplement to the condition of education 2008* (NCES 2008-033.) National Center for Education Statistics, Institute of Education Sciences, U.S. Department of Education, Washington, D.C.

Teranishi, R. (2008). *Asian Americans and Pacific Islanders: Fact Not Fiction—Setting the Record Straight.* New York: The College Board and the National Commission on Asian American and Pacific Islander Research in Education. Retrieved from https://professionals.collegeboard.com/profdownload/08-0608-AAPI.pdf

University of California. (2014). Minutes of the UC Board of Regents. TK

Western Interstate Commission for Higher Education, & Hezel Associates. (2010). *Promising practices in statewide articulation and transfer systems.* Boulder, CO: Western Interstate Commission for Higher Education. Retrieved from www.wiche.edu/info/publications/PromisingPracticesGuide.pdf

Witt, A. A., Wattenbarger, J. L., Gollattscheck, J. F., & Suppiger, J. E. (1994). *America's community colleges: the first century.* Washington, DC: American Association of Community Colleges.

Zakaria, F. (2015). *In defense of a liberal education.* New York: W. W. Norton and Co.

Section I

Strategic Planning

The first two pieces in the strategic planning section are drawn from plenary addresses delivered at the 13th Annual Conference of the National Institute for the Study of Transfer Students in February 2015. Karen Archambault kicks off this section with a well-reasoned plea for the development of a campus culture that embraces the transfer student. Although it is often assumed that such a culture exists by definition on community college campuses, leaders at both two- and four-year institutions would be wise to heed her advice to evaluate the extent to which their programs and services are geared to the needs of transfer students. Mark Allen Poisel goes on to provide recommendations for supporting a specific population of transfer students—student veterans. He argues that institutions need to consider the unique needs and contributions of this diverse and growing student population, comprehensively during their strategic planning processes.

Louise DiCesare extends Archambault's perspective with a perceptive piece that describes the implementation of the "Smart Transfer Plan" within the Minnesota State Colleges and Universities. Spurred by persistent complaints from transfer students, the Minnesota system engaged in a multi-step self-assessment designed to identify and address concerns about the effectiveness of the transfer process in Minnesota. Christopher Hockey at the State University of New York (SUNY) amplifies this topic with a system-wide analysis of policies designed to enhance transfer *within* the SUNY system. By creating an umbrella structure, called "Seamless Transfer," the SUNY system is working to reduce barriers for community college students who wish to earn an associate and bachelor's degrees in four years. From the same system, Erin Rickman and Megan Sarkis at the College of Brockport advance a strategy that takes account of the critical relation between college admission and retention. Understanding that access without support is no guarantee of academic success, their institution engaged in a campus-wide evaluation of the ways in which in which transfer students are served following matriculation.

1

Collaborating Across Campus to Support Transfer Students

Karen Archambault

The annual National Institute for the Study of Transfer Students conference is a unique opportunity for a wide range of professionals to come together with shared purpose. Collectively, members of student affairs and student success offices, registrars and admissions officers, advisors and transfer center staff, academic affairs staff, and faculty, share ideas and gain insights to bring back to their campuses with the hope of making campuses more friendly and welcoming to transfer students. Some attendees are their sole campus representative but they are among friends also focused on the success of transfer students. Some are lucky enough to be one of many transfer advocates on their campuses; others need to work diligently to convince those around them that transfer students are worth the effort necessary for their success. This conference, this organization, and this keynote are about that work.

I first became acquainted with NISTS in 2009, attending and presenting at a conference not unlike the one held in Atlanta in 2015. While there, a statement made by another presenter struck me. She said, "Transfer is the movement of credit from one institution to another." In hearing this statement, I thought that perhaps I was in the wrong place. "No!," I exclaimed on the inside while I sat quietly in the back of a crowded room. "Transfer is about people! It's about our students!" that little voice inside me screamed. Though we often want to respond only to the most rational sides of ourselves, listening to those little voices may tell us that someone has missed the mark; those voices are important. This is especially true when they remind us that there are those amongst our colleagues who—though they may mean well—are not mindful of the very human experience of transfer students.

However, the sentiments we hear on our campuses may not be far from the attitude that transfer is all about the numbers and the credits. And to some extent, the view of transfer students as something other than human and usually as cash cows—sources of revenue but not worth much additional effort–makes sense. Transfer students do not factor in any of the well-known ranking systems, nor are they included in graduation measures that are frequently considered to be the bar by which institutional success is measured. When transfer students are not part of the measures of success for students, resources (both human and financial) remain elusive.

Despite these challenges, change is becoming more likely as greater and greater numbers of transfer students arrive on our campuses. Within one six-year monitoring period, over a third of students (thirty-five percent) attended two or more institutions, including those who transferred vertically, horizontally, swirled between institutions, or simultaneously enrolled (Simone, 2014). While slightly more than half (fifty-six percent) transferred vertically from community colleges to senior institutions, the remainder had other enrollment patterns (Simone, 2014). Just as importantly as these raw numbers, these students are successful: of community college students who transfer, sixty percent attain their bachelor's degrees within six years (Shapiro el al., 2013). Even without representation in the rankings, the greater presence of transfer students on campus forces the transfer issue, because as they arrive on campus, the campus is forced to be responsive. With the increased enrollment of transfer students on campus, now is the right time for transfer advocates to find allies and to make a clear statement regarding the important role of transfer students on our campuses.

Transfer advocates must find allies. While collegiality, cooperation, and collaboration sound like buzzwords, it is essential that advocates live these values to effectively partner with others around campus and across institutional lines. In order to do so, we must recognize the need to think differently. Albert Einstein said, "We cannot solve our problems with the same thinking we used when we created them," and certainly this is true of managing transfer concerns on campus (Einstein, n.d.). For many years, transfer concerns focused on the transfer of credit through articulation agreements and transfer plans. To address the challenges of transfer between institutions as we encourage allies to work with us, we must collectively recognize the need for articulation and transfer agreements but simultaneously move beyond these credit-focused approaches.

In this effort as a campus community, perhaps the place to start is to answer a seemingly simple question: is our campus transfer-friendly and, if not, how do we improve it? Answering this question sets the stage for the rest of the conference and, for most, answering this question involves a willingness to work hard at considering and changing campus culture. The remainder of this talk focuses on this and similar questions, and on the conversations we can encourage to change the transfer student paradigm around our campuses.

First, each transfer student advocate must think about how much buy-in is already present on campus. Buy-in starts with having advocates at the table where decisions that impact transfer students are made. Advocates should think, too, about others at this table. What do those in positions of authority believe about transfer students, their needs, and their experiences? How do these beliefs play out in transfer student experiences with admissions, financial support, orientation, advising, or other services as they enter campus? The answers to these questions frame the experiences that students have and inform our thoughts about how campus culture might need to change or shift.

This campus culture is perhaps most evident where discussions about students are already taking place. Regardless of the area in which a transfer advocate works, the sense of how central the transfer experience is to the mission of the department and the institution influences our work. Transfer students and their concerns can be considered "mission critical" when they are a part of student success discussions and at equal or at least near-equal status with "native" students. Perhaps as importantly, transfer students are mission critical when such discussions do not depend upon who is present in the room, and no specific transfer advocate is necessary because all share a view regarding the importance of transfer students.

When transfer students are mission critical, campus resource allocations reflect care for the needs of these students. Transfer specific programs pervade such campuses, and include transfer-specific orientations and support and mentoring interventions designed for transfer students' progress. These campuses recognize that transfer students will become integrated into campus over time, but high-quality transfer campuses also recognize that such a change does not happen overnight; even students who desperately want to integrate may require additional support. Programs on these campuses are transfer-specific and designed as such, rather than as shortened versions of first-year programs. Simply removing items from a first-year program and calling it "designed" for transfer students feeds into the perception that what transfer students need is identifiable only as being shorter and more concentrated than first-year students. The distinctions between transfer students and freshmen are larger than their greater likelihood to need to accommodate work, families, or other obligations. Institutions that view transfer students as mission critical make the focus of their programming reflective of the unique characteristics of their particular transfer profile.

The demand for a campus culture that views the success of transfer students as mission critical is, at least to some extent, reliant upon the involvement and support of leadership on campus. When leaders' actions demonstrate inclusion of transfer students and appreciation of the challenges these students face during this transition, these students are more likely to experience a campus that welcomes them. When leadership demands the campus reflect an attitude of embracing transfer students, rather than relying on such students as enrollment-boosting cash cows, students experience a campus that bolsters their success. Alternatively, if leadership on campus is resistant to moving transfer students off the sidelines, transfer advocates may expect to encounter additional challenges.

Assuming the campus culture strives to be transfer-friendly, even if it is not yet meeting that standard, the second step in creating a truly transfer-focused campus is to evaluate the student experience. Transfer advocates should consider the part of the student experience in which they have influence, be it the admissions process, orientation, student engagement, or academics. In determining whether the intention of a transfer-friendly campus is truly "lived" on campus, advocates must ask how students experience the campus. Are resources available for specific transfer student programs? For example, when planning admissions events or orientations, transfer-friendly campuses plan for first-year and transfer students simultaneously, rather than planning a transfer student experience with the funds and people who remain after first-year student planning is completed. Determine whether such programs exist on campus at all, as only after identifying these programs can transfer advocates determine whether the resources needed for these programs are available and whether the student experience reflects the distinct needs of transfer students.

On most campuses, whether or not the campus will be inclusive is dependent upon the emphasis given to the transfer experience by those in campus leadership positions. Transfer advocates must find leaders on campus who talk about the campus's students in a comprehensive way that includes transfer students. Leadership on transfer-friendly campuses understands the challenges that such students face at the institution, and works to overcome and dismantle the barriers they may face. When advocates perceive resistance to improving the transfer experience, looking to campus leadership is an excellent way to determine what improvements might be possible.

For many transfer advocates, improving the transfer experience can seem insurmountable; but in reality, there is room on every campus for improvement and collaboration and this is the point of the National Institute for the Study of Transfer Students conference. The intention is not always something entirely new, but to determine what might be new or well suited for a particular campus. For some institutions, massive cultural change is needed while others only require tweaking around the edges. Either way, attendees of the conference should challenge the status quo and suggest the changes—big or small—that benefit the transfer students on his or her campus.

REFERENCES

Einstein, A. (n.d.). BrainyQuote.com. Retrieved from BrainyQuote.com website: http://www.brainyquote.com/quotes/quotes/a/alberteins121993.html

Shapiro, D., Dundar, A., Ziskin, M., Chiang, Y. Chen, J., Torres, V., & Harrell, A. (2013). *Baccalaureate attainment: A national view of the postsecondary outcomes of students who transfer from two-year to four-year institutions* (Signature Report No. 5). Herndon, VA: National Student Clearinghouse Research Center.

Simone, S.A. (2014). *Transferability of postsecondary credit following student transfer or co-enrollment* (NCES 2014-163). U.S. Department of Education. Washington, DC: National Center for Education Statistics. Retrieved from http://nces.ed.gov/pubsearch.

Karen Archambault *is the executive director of enrollment management at Rowan College at Burlington County.*

2

Supporting Student Veterans: The Next Wave

Mark Allen Poisel

Introduction

Many words come to mind when describing student veterans and their experience: military, veteran, student, male, female, young, old, invisible, respected, adjustment, transition, new environment, experience, challenge, different, motivated, no structure, learning disability, and post-traumatic stress disorder. These are simple words that take on very different meanings when associated with student veterans.

Higher education has shifted dramatically. Years ago all students were lumped into the same pot and the mentality was "sink or swim." Then the focus shifted to retention and graduation, with a subsequent realization of a need to be more intentional.

Institutions began to think about the first-year experience, the transfer experience, the sophomore experience, and the senior experience. There is increased programming for special populations. It is with this more nuanced awareness that a sensitivity towards the veteran student experience has begun to evolve.

Veteran Student Experience

Institutions tend to generalize populations. However, this does not work with the diverse subpopulation of student veterans.

Some student veterans want to be invisible. They do not want anyone to know that they were ever in the military. Other veterans are very proud of their military experience, and they want the campus to be proud of it with them. Some veterans are struggling because of their military experience. Other veterans have never seen combat but they are still veterans. Veterans include both men and women, and their experience during and after their service is different. The student veteran population presents with complexity and rich diversity, and similar to transfer students, there are few exact and right answers. How do institutions foster success in such a broad spectrum of students?

On our campuses, student veterans are frequently experiencing personal transitions as they simultaneously assimilate into our local and university environments, and often, their transitions are similar to that of other students. Institutions want to create a welcoming student environment for all students and "invite" all types of students to campus to pursue their educational goals. Transfer, returning adult, and non-traditional students all experience some sort of transition into a new environment.

Institutions have to remember that for student veterans this is not a single transition that is happening, but that there are numerous layers of transition occurring simultaneously.

NAVIGATING A NEW ENVIRONMENT

A student veteran's first six months are as critical as the first six months of any student. Student veterans need orientation and they need help. However, their needs are not the same as other student populations. As noted in The Chronicle of Higher Education, "Veterans especially need help in the first six months to a year, as they move from a high-stress, highly-structured environment into a looser one at college…Colleges should reach out to the veterans arriving on their campuses and help them make the transition from the combat zone to college" (Mytelka, 2010).

Student veterans are unique and this must be kept in mind during planning and service delivery. On many campuses, student veterans are seen as nontraditional students, yet some of them are as young as nineteen or twenty years old. Student veterans are bringing real life experiences into the classroom, however they may also bring different learning styles. For many veterans, this may be their first experience in a college classroom, and many of them did not plan to attend college in the first place.

Student veterans want to go to college, but may find themselves in an environment they aren't fully prepared to experience. Unfortunately, student veterans may not be ready for traditional university teaching and learning. It is possible that for student veterans learning styles have changed because of their experience in the military where the methodological approach is quite different from most of our college classrooms. Many student veterans are used to structured environments, but faculty frequently operate in an unstructured format, and expectations may seem vague. Furthermore, it is unlikely that any two faculty members will conduct their classroom in the same way.

Most colleges and universities aren't truly ready for student veterans. Unless faculty and staff worked with a nearby base or had an existing institutional relationship, institutions generally assume military or student veterans are like any other student. Rarely have student veterans been an integral component of a robust recruitment plan, and in many cases institutions still don't know how to recruit them very well. Most institutions haven't adjusted their marketing materials or websites. Institutions are still struggling to recruit transfer students, and most are not set up to recruit student veterans. In most marketing campaigns, colleges utilize pictures of eighteen-year- olds engaged in a traditional college experience. It is time to do things differently.

Student veterans need to be an intentional part of recruitment instead of backfill designed to increase enrollment numbers and tuition revenue. Colleges and universities must have the necessary resources in place to serve this important student population. Academic assistance offices must be prepared to provide necessary learning support, whether it is academic preparation or accommodations for learning disabilities. Faculty and staff must be prepared to manage the physical and mental challenges that some veterans face. Today's student veterans come with a desire and passion to learn and we must be ready to commit the necessary resources or assistance to help them succeed.

The Student Veterans of Today

Student veterans want a community. They want to belong. They want to connect. Whether it's with other veterans, other students, faculty or staff, they want to be a part of a community. Many student veterans want the reassurance that it's going to be okay, that they can do it, particularly those that didn't receive college prep in high school. Some student veterans may have a GED or may have taken a couple of online courses, and those students especially need encouragement. Student veterans want to be accepted, just like any other student on campus. Sometimes, they just want to be a student.

Sometimes student veterans want to be a part of specialized activities on campus, sometimes they want to interact with other students in a similar situation, and sometimes they want to fly under the radar and be a student like everyone else. Faculty, staff, and administrators have to find a way to help these students achieve their goals. Working with student veterans also informs our knowledge of transfer students.

Student veterans navigate a transition into college life that is similar to transfers and adult learners. But the transition for student veterans is a little bit different, because of a tendency towards a primary identification with military service rather than as an individual. At colleges and universities, the focus is on the individual student as autonomous and independent. Faculty expect students to evaluate, explore, and discuss, and this is quite different from the military experience. It may also be difficult for student veterans to relate to traditional college students, especially the seventeen or eighteen-year-old enrolled in their first general education course.

A challenging transitional moment may occur when a student veteran is sitting in class and other students make political comments, comments about the government, or comments about conflicts or wars. How do veterans process comments that challenge their prior experiences? Student veterans have had life-altering experiences that may make it hard to relate to an eighteen-year-old more interested in the fraternity party on Saturday night than academics. Student veterans may need to be encouraged to socialize within the academic culture of the institution and provided assistance to help them navigate university policies, procedures, campus, and faculty.

Planning and Resources

As institutions focus on intentionally growing their student veteran population, administrators need to consider how they will intentionally foster the student veteran experience on their campuses. Resources and funding tend to follow priorities. If student veterans are going to be a part of an institutional recruitment strategy, resources need to be allocated to help them be successful. A strategic enrollment plan should be designed with the end in mind to assure student veterans are successful.

In order to create student experiences that will be valuable for student veterans, administrators should first seek to respect these students and not treat them like a traditional eighteen-year-old first-year student just out of high school. Faculty and administrators need to consider how they might build programs and services that meet the specific needs of this population. Sometimes nothing additional is needed, and in other instances, programs need to be developed that foster an environment that promotes student success. There must be respect for student veterans' past experience to help assure a successful transition and future.

One way many institutions begin this process is to gather a group of faculty, staff, and students to envision and create new and distinctive programs for student veterans. In this process, it is essential to involve the right people and to create a shared understanding that one person in the veterans and military affairs office cannot be expected to resolve all of the issues for student veterans. Most faculty and staff approach this challenge with good intentions, but lack the understanding of how to build the right experience. Individuals want to do the right thing, but often forget to take the time to evaluate the situation and ask the right questions, as the issues are frequently more complex than previously realized. Intentional and well-developed planning can make all of the difference in how a successful program is designed and implemented.

Finally, university faculty and staff should consider how to help student veterans understand the need to avail themselves of resources and assistance. Universities have policies that impact the benefits, aid, and graduation of student veterans, and student veterans may need to be encouraged to seek assistance to benefit from the programs or services provided. Student veterans may want to be invisible, but institutions have a responsibility to make sure each student veteran knows that if they hit a roadblock or obstacle, there is someone at the institution to help them who will respect them and their circumstances.

RECOMMENDATIONS

Institutions need to create a safe and comfortable "home" space for student veterans. The concept of "coming home" has a powerful impact. Student veteran centers can become a safe place to return to whenever life and situations get really tough and there is a need for comfort and connection.

It is important to foster a community that attracts student veterans. This sense of community should extend beyond the campus and involve the programs, services, and activities in the local area. The additional outreach allows faculty and administrators to engage others in students' success. Many campuses host a week of appreciation, special recognition days, inclusive programming, or find other ways to teach the campus community about student veterans and their experiences.

It is also important to consider institutional goals for veteran students' success. As an institution, faculty and administrators frequently discuss different services and initiatives, and these conversations need to return to a central vision focused on the success of the student. To assure the success of student veterans, institutions need to train and hire staff that understand war and/or are willing to learn. Partnerships are needed to develop programs in a veteran-friendly institution, because no one faculty or staff member will be able to achieve the goals alone. Collaboration can be tough, and meeting the challenge of reaching a consensus on what is most needed—or how the plan will develop and work–is the best way to provide support to students.

All veteran-friendly institutions must develop an appropriate veteran orientation program. This orientation should not be the same two-day, first-year program with an extra hour at the end for information about VA benefits. Rather, this orientation must be a different kind of program, perhaps more similar to a transfer or non-traditional student program. This may be an online orientation that enhances existing campus programming, but whatever is created, the best way to develop the program is to evaluate the needs and wants of student veterans. Consult with your current student veterans to assist in program design decisions. There may be resistance to creating a new orientation program, but it is important to remember that student veterans must navigate your college or university's unique bureaucracy. Orientation is a common practice whether starting a new job, joining a new gym, or beginning a military experience. If the term *Orientation* is a concern, then name it something else. Use whatever term works best, but provide a formal way for student veterans to initiate the process of assimilating to your institution.

Conclusion

As institutions review and assess their programs and services, there are several questions campus administrators should consider in developing the strategy for helping student veterans.

- What challenges will student veterans face on campus?
- What needs and wants do they bring to campus?
- What programs and services are needed?
- Should we provide separate/supplemental support services?
- What resources will be needed for student veterans?
- How will the prioritization of resources be determined?
- How will the entire campus community be engaged?
- Where do opportunities for collaboration exist?

These questions allow campus organizing committees to evaluate their needs and to create a strategic plan with intentional initiatives and a timeline that coincides with available resources.

Finally, there are key elements that help to assure veteran students' success. As campuses focus on student veterans, there are simple steps to initiate the process.

- Develop a vision and plan for student veterans
- Hire and train student veteran-friendly staff

- Partner with faculty, staff, and student veterans to maintain institutional support
- Build a communication system that involves both internal and external partners
- Prepare veterans to become students
- Develop a student veteran appropriate orientation program
- Develop specific policies and procedures

As institutions contemplate how to help student veterans, serious questions must be addressed concerning what campus resources may be provided to student veterans. How are programs, services, and resources going to be designed that help student veterans succeed? Repeatedly defining what student veteran success is on your campus will help in the planning and implementation of effective programs.

Discussions and planning are happening on college and university campuses that will begin or continue to encourage alternative methods for serving this very important and growing subpopulation of our student veterans. Student veterans are complex and unique. They may be complicated, but they are valuable to our campuses and demand our respect. Student veterans need to be remembered at the start, not as an afterthought. We need to build our enrollment, retention, and progression programs with the success of our student veterans in mind.

References

Mytelka, A. (2010). Colleges should help veterans on path to new future, VA secretary says. *The Chronicle of High Education.*

Mark Allen Poisel *is the vice president for enrollment and student affairs at Augusta University.*

3

Implementation of the Smart Transfer Plan

Louise DiCesare

Organizational Description

The Minnesota State Colleges and Universities (MnSCU) is a public system of twenty-four two-year community, comprehensive, and technical colleges and seven state universities. The two-year colleges award Associate of Arts, Associate of Science, Associate of Fine Arts, Associate of Applied Science, diplomas and certificates. The state universities award baccalaureate, master's and applied doctorate degrees. The two-year colleges are open admission, although some programs are selective. State universities select students among qualified applicants. This public state college and university system called the Minnesota State Colleges and Universities enrolls over 430,000 students. There is a system office that oversees the thirty-one colleges and universities and is responsible for implementing system policies and procedures.

Statement of the Issue

Due to ongoing complaints about transfer, a survey was sent to students who had transferred into an MnSCU system college or university in 2010. The survey was jointly sponsored by the Minnesota State College Student Association (MSCSA), the Minnesota Student University Student Association (MSUSA) and the system office. The survey was administered between January and March 2010 to 9,878 students who had transferred during the fall semester, 2008. A total of 1,023 students responded (about 10%).

Findings from the 2010 survey included the following:

- One third (34%) of respondents rated their transfer experience as fair or poor twenty-three percent (23%) fair and eleven percent (11%) poor).

- About one quarter (24%) said their transfer experience did not meet their expectations.
- A significant number of students (40%) did not seek advice or planned for transfer too late (41%) to make good academic decisions.
- Students were much more likely to use campus-specific websites than the MnSCU system transfer website.
- Sixty-seven percent (67%) of respondents were not aware of the transfer appeal process, which provides students with an opportunity to have their courses re-evaluated for transfer credit if originally denied by the receiving institution.

These 2010 findings led to the development of the following recommendations to improve transfer:

- Develop uniform and ongoing training of transfer advisors.
- Clarify the use of syllabi, course outlines, or other equivalency documents
- Review and improve messaging about the transfer process.
- Improve marketing of the MnSCU system tools and resources to assist with transfer. These tools include Degree Audit Reporting System (DARS) audits, use of Transferology®, and the www.mn-transfer.org (Minnesota Transfer.org) website.
- Increase awareness of the transfer appeal process.
- Increase staff at the system office (another full time position was added in January, 2011).
- Assure accuracy of and compliance with course equivalency data using electronic tools.

These recommendations led to the creation of the Smart Transfer Plan in 2010. To assess the effectiveness of this plan, a follow-up survey was administered December through January, 2013-2014 with the findings and results reported below.

PROGRAM DESCRIPTION

Current State of Transfer in Minnesota

Transfer students make up a growing number of new enrollees at Minnesota State Colleges and Universities. At two-year colleges, students transferring from another college or university represented twenty-five percent (25%) of all new enrollees in 2013, up from twenty-one percent (21%) in 2008. At state universities, transfer students, although fewer in number than at two-year colleges, constituted forty-two percent (42%) of all newly enrolled students in 2013, up from thirty-nine percent (39%) in 2008. In 2013, there were 33,254 transfer students. Sixty percent of them, or 19,983, transferred from one MnSCU college or university to another.

History of the Minnesota Transfer Curriculum

The increasing number of transfer students in Minnesota in the early 1990s led the state public systems to develop the Minnesota Transfer Curriculum (MnTC) as a way of streamlining general education across two- and four-year public institutions in the state.

When first developed, this forty-credit, ten-goal area package of courses addressed the transfer of lower division general education requirements at all Minnesota public higher education institutions (MnSCU and the University of Minnesota). The original legislation stipulated that students who completed the *entire* transfer curriculum and had this achievement recorded on their transcript were deemed to have met all general education requirements for the baccalaureate degree. In 2001, however, an omnibus bill (Minnesota Session Laws, 2001) amended this requirement to allow students to apply any portion of the MnTC completed at the sending institution to apply towards general education requirements at an MnSCU receiving institution. In other words, transfer students who completed MnTC courses could apply that coursework toward general education requirements at the receiving MnSCU institution. Also, if a student completed one or more of the ten goal areas at one MnSCU college or university, those corresponding goal areas would be considered complete at all MnSCU institutions. (This 2001 law, however, did not apply to the University of Minnesota.)

Despite these and other enhancements, state legislators continued to hear complaints and initiated an audit of the transfer process in 2009.

Concurrent with the audit and in order to identify the most problematic areas, the Minnesota State College Student Association (MSCSA), Minnesota State University Student Association (MSUSA) and the system office developed a survey of transfer students in 2010. Results from this survey led to a series of recommendations to improve transfer dubbed the "Smart Transfer Plan." This plan required all Minnesota public colleges and universities to:

- Post course outlines for all courses on their institutional websites with a link to the system transfer website (Course Schedule, Outlines, Catalogs);

- Evaluate each other's courses (within the MnSCU system) in advance and enter the information in DARS so students would know how courses transfer and apply to programs before they take them;

- Provide students with information about how to appeal transfer course/credit decisions for which they disagree;

- Increase staff training by adding regional transfer meetings (to supplement the existing annual Transfer Specialist Conference and Transfer Orientation); and

- Post a transfer page on the college/university website, improve communication about transfer, and improve advising strategies. The website transfer page should include links to the current college or university MnTC/AA degree, national test information (AP, CLEP, IB, and DSST), a link to Transferology ® (the system articulation agreement database), and transfer policies and advising information.

Soon after completion of the survey, implementation of the Smart Transfer Plan began in 2010. Immediate changes included online posting of course outlines on college and university websites with a link to the system transfer website; articulation of all courses from other colleges/universities throughout the system; and increased communication to students about the transfer appeal process.

At the end of 2013, a second survey was administered (and sponsored by the same entities that initiated the first survey in 2010) to assess the productivity of the transfer process since implementation of the Smart Transfer Plan. The survey was administered to 18,768 students who had transferred into a MnSCU system college or university. A total of 1,543 students (8%) completed the survey. The results of the survey revealed broad improvements and continuing challenges. Main findings for the 2013-2014 survey included the following:

- Thirty-five percent (35%) of respondents completed the Minnesota Transfer Curriculum prior to transfer in 2013 compared to thirty percent (30%) in 2010;

- Twenty-five percent (25%) of respondents completed MnTC courses or goal areas in 2013 compared to twenty-four percent (24%) in 2010;

- Fifty-five percent (55%) of respondents completed an Associate of Arts, Associate of Science, Associate of Applied Science, bachelor's degree, certificate, or diploma compared to forty-three percent (43%) in 2010;

- Eighty-one percent (81%) of respondents said transfer of general education/MnTC met or exceeded expectations compared to seventy-six percent (76%) in 2010. Of these, seventeen percent (17%) indicated the MnTC *exceeded* expectations compared to eleven percent (11%) in 2010.

- Eighty percent (80%) of respondents indicated that the transfer process was easier than expected or met their expectations compared to seventy-four (74%) in 2010. Of these, thirty-nine percent (39%) said the process was easier compared to twenty-eight percent (28%) in 2010.

- Seventy-six percent (76%) of respondents rated their overall satisfaction of transfer as "good" or "excellent" compared to sixty-six percent (66%) in 2010. Of these, twenty-seven percent (27%) rated satisfaction "excellent" compared to twenty-one percent (21%) in 2010.

- Sixty-three percent (63%) of respondents sought advice for transfer from a variety of sources compared to sixty percent (60%) in 2010. In 2013, forty-six percent (46%) of respondents met with a counselor or advisor whereas sixty-nine percent (69%) sought advice from these sources in 2010;

- Thirty-eight percent (38%) of respondents were aware of the transfer appeal process compared to thirty-three percent (33%) in 2010;

- Of all the comments provided, twenty-five percent (25%) were complaints about advising and information compared to thirty percent (30%) in 2010;

- Thirteen percent (13%) of all comments included complaints about loss of credits compared to twenty-two percent (22%) in 2010;

- Two percent (2%) of comments included complaints about transcript issues compared to eight percent (8%) in 2010;

- Reported use of current institutional website was seventy-eight percent (78%) in 2010 and fifty-three percent (53%) in 2013;

- Reported use of last college/university website was fifty-nine percent (59%) in 2010 and thirty-seven percent (37%) in 2013;

- Reported use of system website (www.MnTransfer.org) stayed roughly the same with twenty-two percent (22%) using it in 2010 and twenty-one percent (21%) in 2013; and

- The reported use of u.select® (now Transferology®) was six percent (6%) in 2010 and ten percent (10%) in 2013.

LESSONS LEARNED

The Smart Transfer Plan likely contributed to some improvements in transfer in Minnesota, although causation cannot be assumed. Given the plan's high visibility, for example, faculty and staff at colleges and universities throughout the state increased their attention to transfer, which also likely contributed to improved transfer outcomes.

Several system wide elements of the Smart Transfer Plan appear to be especially effective. For example, creating and distributing course outlines has increased the degree and speed to which two- and four-year institutions can evaluate courses for applicability towards degree requirements. (Even non-system institutions are using these course outlines to help evaluate courses). The proliferation of course outlines has led to an increase in the number of courses evaluated in advance for transfer, entered into DARS, and made visible in Transferology® to help students and advisors with transfer planning.

Students also have greater access to accurate transfer information on-line. In addition, students' awareness of transfer appeals has increased somewhat, yet work remains to make further improvements. Currently, a new technology-based approach is being developed to appear in the registration portal that will capture student inquiries and appeals about transfer and will allow for the analysis of students' questions and concerns about the transfer process. It is anticipated that this process will encourage students to review how their courses/credits transferred sooner and meet with staff to better understand how their courses/credits are evaluated.

RECOMMENDATIONS AND LIMITATIONS

Not all aspects of the Smart Transfer Plan can be definitively assessed. For example, it is difficult to determine the extent to which colleges and universities have evaluated one another's courses. Another challenge is that a few campuses initially resisted posting a transfer page web link on their website homepage; however, they are all currently doing so. The fact that transfer students now exceed first-time students may help to bring the necessary attention to make ongoing enhancements to the transfer process.

REFERENCES

MinnesotaTransfer.org. Retrieved from http://www.mntransfer.org/

Minnesota Transfer. *Minnesota transfer curriculum.* Retrieved from http://www.mntransfer.org/students/plan/s_mntc.php

Minnesota Transfer. *Course schedule, outlines, catalogs.* Retrieved from http://www.mntransfer.org/students/plan/s_schedules.php

The Office of the Revisor of Statutes. (2001). *2001 Minnesota session law.* Retrieved from https://www.revisor.mn.gov/laws/?year=2001&-type=1&group=Session+Law&doctype=Chapter&id=1&keyword_type=exact&keyword=internet-based+student+manual

The Office of the Revisor of Statutes. (2010). *2010 Minnesota session law.* Retrieved from https://www.revisor.mn.gov/laws/?year=2010&-type=0&group=Session+Law&doctype=Chapter&id=364&keyword_type=exact&keyword=identify+discrepancies+in+transferring+and+-accepting+credits

The Office of the Revisor of Statutes. (2011). *2011 Minnesota session laws.* Retrieved from https://www.revisor.mn.gov/laws/?year=2011&-type=1&group=Session+Law&doctype=Chapter&id=5&keyword_type=exact&keyword=systems+smart+transfer+plan

Transferology. (2015). Retrieved from https://www.transferology.com/state/mn

INSTITUTIONAL DESCRIPTION

Name and Location:
The Minnesota State Colleges and Universities, Minnesota

Institution Type:
State university system consisting of public two- and four-year institutions

Institutional Selectivity:
Open admissions and varying levels of selectivity

Size of Enrollment:
Over 430,000

Louise DiCesare *is the system director for transfer and collaboration at the Minnesota State Colleges and Universities system.*

4

TECHNOLOGY AND TRANSFER: SUNY'S INTEGRATION OF TRANSFER POLICY AND TECHNOLOGY

Christopher Hockey

STATEMENT OF THE ISSUE

SUNY is one of the largest university systems in the United States, and provides policy, vision, and support to its sixty-four campuses. One of the most recent priorities of system administration has been to study transfer student mobility and success, examining what policies and systems could be established to support these initiatives system-wide across all sixty-four campuses.

SHORT OVERVIEW

In an effort to increase the ability for students in the SUNY system to transfer within SUNY seamlessly without loss of credit, the State University of New York began to develop system-wide policies and implement system-wide technology ("2014 State of the University Address," 2014). Seamless Transfer, an umbrella term used to describe all the policies that support SUNY transfer, has provided a solid policy foundation for students in SUNY to earn an associate's degree and a bachelor's degree within four years ("2014 State of the University Address," 2014). In addition, the implementation of DegreeWorks and TransferFinder have provided technological tools that allow students to view their degree progress from their current campus or if they transferred to any another campus in the SUNY system. Importantly, a grant provided by the Lumina Foundation ("Lumina", 2015) allowed SUNY to develop infrastructure and procedures to award associate's degrees to students who have transferred to a four-year campus without earning the associate's degree first.

PROGRAM DESCRIPTION

There are four major components of SUNY's efforts to improve transfer student mobility and success. The first component is a collection of SUNY-wide policies labeled as "seamless transfer." Seamless transfer comprises a standardized general education curriculum and a set of foundational courses for each of the most popular majors across the university system ("2014 State of the University Address," 2014). The foundational courses are labeled as "transfer pathways." The transfer pathways were developed by collecting the lower division requirements for all major programs across all sixty-four campuses. These lower division courses were compiled and analyzed in an effort to identify common themes across the system. The end result of the analysis was the creation of thirty-seven transfer paths (fifty-eight majors) in the most popular disciplines ("2014 State of the University Address," 2014). The existing collection of transfer paths covers 95% of all transfer students within SUNY. Each transfer path is made up of the core courses for that major which were defined by soliciting input from over 400 faculty from both two- and four-year campuses ("2014 State of the University Address," 2014). The end result of this project was a collection of nearly 15,000 courses in what is now called the Mobility Database. Critically, these courses are guaranteed to transfer to all SUNY campuses.

The general education component of seamless transfer is foundational, and vital to the success of transfer students. All of the SUNY community colleges must follow the basic general education curriculum that requires students to complete seven out of ten categories and earn thirty credits in those categories. The general education categories include basic communication, math, natural sciences, social sciences, American history, western civilization, foreign language, other world civilization, humanities, and the arts. Students enrolled at four-year campuses in the SUNY system are required to minimally complete the seven out of ten but may also be required to complete additional requirements set forth by the campus. As part of the policy, receiving institutions must accept a category as completed by the sending institution if indicated on the General Education Transcript Addendum. However, this does not mean the course is guaranteed to transfer, simply that the requirement is met. Courses which have as a prerequisite a course approved for SUNY GER are also approvable in that category. Having courses approved in more than one category, and allowing students to meet more than one category with a single course or "double dipping," is allowable according to local campus policy.

An additional component of seamless transfer is the establishment of credit caps on all degree programs. Campuses must limit associate's degree programs to 64 credits and bachelor's degree programs to 126 credits. These limits are significantly under the national average for degree programs and allow for students to complete any degree program–if the correct courses are chosen and completed–within a two or four year timeframe.

Four major policies were implemented in the establishment of seamless transfer for campuses. First, all SUNY A.A and A.S. graduates are guaranteed the transfer of 60 credits of their coursework towards the bachelor's degree ("SUNY Transfer Policies," 2015). Second, students are guaranteed that up to 30 credits of general education courses in the ten subject areas noted above will also transfer ("2014 State of the University Address," 2014). Third, students are guaranteed they will not need to repeat courses with the same (at least 70%) content. Fourth, all students with an A.A. or A.S. are guaranteed transfer to at least one SUNY 4-year campus ("SUNY Transfer Policies," 2015).

While the seamless transfer policies are an important element to the success of transfer students in the SUNY system, they are only effective if students are provided support to remain on track to graduate. The DegreeWorks system provides an interactive degree audit tool for students, and allows students to see their progress towards the completion of their degree. The goal of a system-wide implementation of DegreeWorks is that every SUNY undergraduate student will have comprehensive, interactive degree planning services at every SUNY institution, with the ability for students considering transfer to assess their degree progress at other SUNY institutions.

DegreeWorks is a software application that allows students to view their degree audit directly from their campus portal. Individual campuses enter the degree requirements for each program and as students register for courses they are able to see how those courses apply to their degree program and to their general education requirements. One component of DegreeWorks that SUNY currently pilots is the Transfer Finder application. Transfer Finder allows students to see how their courses would transfer to another institution within the SUNY system. Students have the ability to compare their coursework in three degree programs at up to three institutions, resulting in a total comparison of nine degree programs. Transfer Finder is currently in testing at eighteen SUNY campuses.

The final focus of SUNY's transfer student initiative centers on reverse transfer ("Credit When It's Due," 2015). In 2012, SUNY was a recipient of a $500,000 grant from the Lumina Foundation ("Lumina", 2015). This grant was one of many awarded to several states in an effort to increase the number of students awarded an associate's degree. Lumina's ("Lumina", 2015) goal is to increase the proportion of Americans with high-quality degrees and credentials to 60% by 2025, and this goal was in alignment with SUNY's strategic initiatives for completion and success. SUNY also saw this as an opportunity to expand the functionality of DegreeWorks to include reverse transfer. SUNY chose to allocate the grant funds to create a sustainable infrastructure for a reverse transfer program that would continue beyond the life of the grant.

The major efforts toward the reverse transfer initiative are ongoing, and have centered on developing course equivalencies for those institutions that did not have a working database of articulations. Over a period of two years, SUNY was able to develop over 95,000 course articulations. In addition, SUNY has made major strides towards developing a web presence and FERPA consent form to facilitate the movement of students through a reverse transfer process.

End Result & Impacts/Lessons Learned

All of the initiatives related to mobility and transfer have resulted in positive outcomes as well as lessons learned. The policy changes related to student mobility and transfer have shown to be helpful to students. The Transfer Pathway project has provided all SUNY students with a specific set of courses for the most common majors. The pathway courses in combination with a more standardized general education program have created an environment that encourages students enrolled at SUNY community colleges to complete their general education requirements and progress significantly in their major, thus increasing the likelihood that they will enter the four-year campus as a junior. The alignment of general education and major courses results in more students earning an associate's degree, transferring to a four-year campus, and earning a bachelor's degree.

DegreeWorks has proven to be popular with students and advisors as it is perceived to be user-friendly and informative, more so than any previous versions. While the TransferFinder product is not yet available to students, testing with advisors and registrars has been positive. However, there have been internal challenges with the TransferFinder implementation. In particular, there have been concerns regarding the perception that making it easier for students to identify the best campus to transfer to will result in students leaving their currently enrolled campus. These concerns however have no factual basis. While the transparency that TransferFinder provides is one of the key purposes of the product, there is some concern from individual campuses that this level of transparency will result in a competitive edge for those campuses that are more aligned with SUNY policies and recommendations.

The efforts to create a sustainable reverse transfer process have proved to be the most challenging. The first major hurdle with the proposed process was navigating FERPA regulations, resulting in the development of a website to collect student consent. The second major challenge was with the data collection of student information. Since the collection of individual student emails at the system level didn't exist, a process needed to be developed to collect individual emails from each institution identified. The major lessons learned underscored the challenges of integrating and understanding complex data collection across the system.

RECOMMENDATIONS AND LIMITATIONS

Campuses or university systems interested in implementing new technology to support student mobility should explore several options and speak to current users of the products to gain a better understanding of the challenges associated with each solution. Costs need to be considered when adopting any technology solution, and those costs should be weighed against the functions and features of the potential solution. In addition to the short term costs of software purchases, systems or campuses need to consider the long term costs associated with sustainability of any new technology. Examples of these long term costs include–but are not limited to–additional IT staff required to maintain the technology, additional administrative staff to oversee implementation and continued development of the technology, and any additional hardware needed.

When developing policy to support student mobility and transfer student success, institutions and university systems should collaborate with faculty and appropriate staff. University systems or legislative bodies should focus efforts on developing models of common courses. This can be accomplished through specific common numbering systems or through developing a database of courses that meet learning outcomes for specific programs and general education categories. Individual campuses should identify and work closely with partner institutions to seek to more closely align curriculum between programs.

COST OF THE INITIATIVE AND SOURCE OF FUNDING

The primary funding source for the policy and technology initiatives has been funded via capital funding awarded through the state legislature, as well as from SUNY's budget. The policy changes developed to support student mobility and transfer within SUNY required minimal financial investments, although there were costs related to website development.

In contrast, the DegreeWorks initiative is a sizeable budget item for the System. DegreeWorks was traditionally purchased by individual campuses. However, in an effort to streamline degree auditing across the university system, DegreeWorks was purchased for each of the 64 campuses. In addition to the cost of the baseline DegreeWorks product, there are significant costs associated with hardware and IT staff and support systems. The implementation of the TransferFinder product, which is an additional component of DegreeWorks, did not result in any additional significant costs. There were minimal costs for training and additional IT support.

SUNY received a thirty-month, $500,000 grant from the Lumina Foundation for the Credit When It's Due project ("Credit When It's Due", 2015). These monies largely funded salaries and benefits for professional staff and significant amounts of student staff. In over a two year period, the student staff of two-to-six members was primarily responsible for developing over 95,000 course equivalencies for nineteen campuses in the SUNY System.

REFERENCES

Lumina Foundation. (2015). Retrieved from https://www.luminafoundation.org/

Lumina Foundation. (2015). *Credit when it's due*. Retrieved from https://www.luminafoundation.org/credit-when-its-due

Office of Community College Research and Leadership. (2015). *Credit when it's due*. Retrieved from http://occrl.illinois.edu/projects/cwid/

The State University of New York. (2015). *SUNY transfer policies*. Retrieved from http://www.suny.edu/attend/get-started/transfer-students/suny-transfer-policies/

The State University of New York. (2015). *2014 state of the university address*. Retrieved from http://www.suny.edu/about/leadership/chancellor-nancy-zimpher/speeches/2014-sou/

INSTITUTIONAL DESCRIPTION

Name and Location:
State University of New York (SUNY) System Administration, Albany, NY

Institutional type:
State-operated public community colleges and four-year campuses

Institutional Selectivity:
Varying levels of selectivity

Size of Enrollment:
460,000 system-wide

Christopher L. Hockey *is the associate director of transfer success and technology at the State University of New York (SUNY) Center for Professional Development*

5

FROM PROSPECT TO GRADUATE: PERFECTING THE PARTNERSHIP OF ADMISSIONS AND RETENTION

Erin Rickman and Megan Sarkis

STATEMENT OF THE ISSUE

The College at Brockport has a rich history of admitting and graduating more transfer students than freshmen. From the prospect phase through graduation it is imperative that the college's admissions and retention departments dismantle silos and foster open communication, collaboration, and assessment. In an environment of declining student demographics, the college has adjusted its admissions requirements for new transfer students. Instead of holding a firm line at a minimum GPA of 2.5 for consideration, the College reviews and considers students that show potential for success with slightly lower averages. Accordingly, the offices of admissions and retention communicate the needs of all parties involved with the focus on student success.

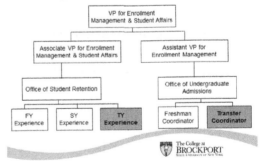

SHORT OVERVIEW

In the spring of 2009, the college created a Transfer-Year Experience Coordinator (TYE) position in Student Retention. The candidate selected for the position brought six years of experience as a transfer admissions coordinator in Undergraduate Admissions. The familiarity with the admissions process has proved to be extremely valuable, especially when creating, implementing, and assessing new transfer student initiatives.

Prior to the creation of the TYE position, the successful transition for transfer students fell primarily into the departments of Undergraduate Admissions and Academic Advisement. Previous strategies included the following:

- Student Orientation Advisement and Registration (SOAR), the primary transition event for new transfer students.

- An Academic Advisor in Residence Life would travel to feeder institutions to meet one-on-one with students planning to attend Brockport. The purpose of the program was to ensure that students were taking the appropriate classes at their current community college.

- An Undergraduate Admissions Advisor and an Academic Advisor team held group sessions for community college students that were undecided about their transfer institution.

Prior to acceptance, the Undergraduate Admissions office was the point of contact for new transfers, and after students accepted an offer of admission, the Academic Advisement office became the point of contact.

The direction of the transfer program and campus support gained momentum in the fall of 2009 with the creation of the TYE program. The College at Brockport accepted an invitation to participate in the 2009-2010 Foundations of Excellence® in the First College Year Transfer Focus, a project directed by the Policy Center on the First Year of College (a constituent unit of the John N. Gardner Institute for Excellence in Undergraduate Education). Through the College's involvement with the Foundations of Excellence® and the work of the College's Transfer Task Force (2007), the institution implemented the position with various responsibilities including:

- Assist incoming transfer students as they transition to the College

- Promote early relationships among new transfer students and current students, and between new transfer student and the college community

- Familiarize students and their families with campus resources and services

Thus, the TYE coordinator creates and facilitates orientation for new transfer students, creates and coordinates the Transfer Peer Mentor program, creates and facilitates the Transfer Academic Planning Seminar (TAPS), helps to establish a chapter of the honor society Tau Sigma, creates and facilitates recruitment initiatives, administers a probation program for second semester transfer students, as well as develops and facilitates semi-annual Transfer Professional Workshops for regional community college advisors.

PROGRAM DESCRIPTION

The College understands the positive impact of connecting students to available resources as quickly as possible. With the creation of the TYE position, there was also now an institutional acknowledgement that it was important to have transfer students also intentionally connected to resources, especially when considering the condensed time transfer students spend at the college in comparison to direct entry students. Keeping this in mind, the TYE Coordinator constructed a set of programmatic outcomes focused on creating these connections.

Students who participate in TYE programs will:

- Integrate into the college seamlessly and begin to exhibit class affinity and college affiliation
- Declare major and formulate career goals
- Negotiate the faculty advisement system in a timely manner
- Identify campus services
- Negotiate the course management system (Blackboard) and navigate BANNER
- Explain Degree Audit
- Describe instructors' expectations
- Identify a faculty/staff member as a "go-to person"
- Develop a supportive peer group

Utilizing the expertise of the College's research analyst, we are able to track students' progress, and confirmed that connecting new transfer students helps them become more successful in terms of retention. For example, preliminary data shows that students who took the Transfer Academic Planning Seminar GEP 300 were re-

Transfer Academic Planning Seminar (TAPS) GEP 300 Retention Data				
			% Retained	
Cohort	GEP 300 n	ALL n	GEP 300	All
Fall 2009	10	878	80%	78%
Fall 2010	30	946	83%	76%
Fall 2011	45	882	84%	74%
Fall 2012	65	899	91%	70%
Fall 2013	73	868	85%	64%
Fall 2014	95	897	91%	77%

tained to the next year at greater rates than the overall cohort, and the gap appears to be widening.

The declining demographics in WNY and the subsequent lowering of admissions requirements for new transfer students, make it imperative that admissions and retention work together. This data helps to underscore the importance of this collaboration. The admissions and retention offices collaborate on a number of programs including–but not limited to–the following programs:

- The college's Visitation Team brings together a cadre of professional staff from admissions, advisement, financial aid, residential life, and retention to meet with our counterparts at our feeder institutions. This proves to be a simple way to open the doors of communication with the college's feeder institutions.

- Transfer Fridays is a recruitment program that assists prospective, accepted and/or deposited transfer students as they navigate the application and admissions process, review potential credit evaluation, and connect with transfer specific resources. This occurs before the student officially begins their journey at the College.

- The transfer of responsibility for transfer students occurs from Undergraduate Admissions to Student Retention once the student places their deposit and commits to attending the college.

    - Once Student Retention receives notice that students have deposited (weekly reports) the office mails a "Brockport Bound" postcard. The postcard instructs students to access the "transfer student checklist" that outlines their next steps on our Brockport Bound website.

    - Students receive information regarding their mandatory online orientation at this time. Provided via Blackboard, the online orientation is designed to communicate the resources available to students at the College. This helps to assure information is easily available to our transfer students early in their transition.

    - Students that may need additional assistance or have only provisionally met admissions requirements receive direct marketing materials encouraging their enrollment in the transfer academic seminar. With students that have met lower admissions standards, professionals in Undergraduate Admissions and Student Retention communicate to the student recognition of their academic potential and the potential need for additional resources.

- Transfer Professional Workshops provide the college's colleagues from feeder institutions updates regarding their students' performance, undergraduate admissions requirements and data (applications, accepts, deposits, etc.) as well as updates from academic advisement. Each semester, Student Retention hosts transfer professionals to discuss a specific major, transfer student performance in that major and how their transfer students compare to direct entry students.

END RESULTS

The College has seen a vast improvement in the communication between the offices of Student Retention and Undergraduate Admissions since the completion of the Foundations of Excellence® in the First Year and Transfer Focus study, creation of TYE coordinator position, and the creation/implementation of transfer specific programming. Communication continues to open doors to the creation and modification of transfer student specific programming. The College currently boasts a 77% first-to-second-year retention rate for the Fall 2014 transfer student cohort.

RECOMMENDATIONS AND LIMITATIONS

The College at Brockport continues to investigate various recommendations and possibilities for refinement and improvement. The overarching limitation remains resources. Possible future programming might include:

- Imbedded recruitment piece at feeders?
- Mandatory TAPS?
- Parent and family programs for transfer students?
- Overnight visitation/orientation experience for transfer students?
- Transfer student specific programming for campus community?
- Further Veteran programing?

REFERENCES

The College at Brockport. (2015). Undergraduate admissions fall/spring enrollment targets report, provided through the college's Operations Office.

The College at Brockport. (2011). The college's strategic plan 2011-2016. Retrieved from https://www.brockport.edu/planning/2011/

INSTITUTIONAL DESCRIPTION

Name and Location:
The College at Brockport, State University of New York (SUNY)

Institution Type:
Public four-year comprehensive

Institutional Selectivity:
Moderately competitive

Size of Enrollment:
7,000

Erin Rickman *is the transfer year experience coordinator at the College at Brockport, State University of New York (SUNY).*

Megan Sarkis *is the assistant director of undergraduate admissions at the College at Brockport, State University of New York (SUNY).*

SECTION II

CURRICULAR INNOVATIONS AND INITIATIVES

This section includes innovative advances in curricula designed to serve transfer students at two- and four-year institutions. Learning communities, for example, are a well-known innovation, receiving considerable attention in the literature as a strategy for engaging students in faculty-to-student and student-to-student interactions and activities. What is less known, however, is the extent to which such communities may serve the transfer student population. Stephanie Foote and Jean So at Kennesaw State University describe the work of faculty and staff who engaged in an important self-study to assess the extent to which their institution served the needs of transfer students. The result is a set of curricular and co-curricular programs for transfer students, with learning communities at the center of this work.

The work of Carmen Fies and Joseph Kulhanek addresses the persistent shortfall of students—especially traditionally underrepresented students—who choose engineering for their future careers. The product of their efforts is the creation of a Transfer Academy for Tomorrow's Engineer (TATE) program at the University of Texas at San Antonio, with community college partners at Alamo Colleges, Del Mar College, Laredo Community College, and Lone Star College. Their successful cohort-model program is designed to support engineering transfer students with intentional programming focused on improving students' technical writing, presentation, and group work skills in order to prepare graduates for meeting industry demands. Adam Joncich's research also leans heavily on the importance of active learning with "Transfer Star Stories," an innovative fine arts performance program that equips transfer participants with a powerful set of storytelling techniques that illuminate the unique perspectives of community college transfer students.

Finally, Patricia Shea and Catherine Walker at the Western Interstate Commission for Higher Education (WICHE) describe the Interstate Passport Initiative, a "friction-free" framework for the transmission and acceptance of college credits. What is striking about this approach is not simply its ambitious effort to make the transfer process easier for students, but the development of a framework—or curriculum—that students can transport from institution to institution that is rigorous and faithful to the aims of a liberal arts education.

6

FOSTERING SELF-AUTHORSHIP IN THE TRANSFER STUDENT EXPERIENCE THROUGH THE DEVELOPMENT OF A LEARNING COMMUNITY

Stephanie M. Foote and C. Jean So

STATEMENT OF THE ISSUE

Given the number of students transferring to KSU annually, the university engaged in a self-study process that allowed faculty and staff to develop a deeper understanding of the transfer student experience at KSU. As a result of that process, staff in Orientation and Transition Programs (OTP) and faculty in First-Year and Transition Studies (FYTS) were able to create curricular and co-curricular programs for transfer students. One of the programs developed and led by faculty and staff in OTP and FYTS is the transfer student learning community, "Flourishing at KSU," which is the focus of this paper.

SHORT OVERVIEW

Institutional data collected through the self-study process and student development theory informed the development of the transfer student learning community at KSU. The focus of the learning community was to provide new transfer students with experiences and opportunities to self-author by examining personal strengths, interests, skills, knowledge, and information needed to be successful in a major and/or chosen career as well as through engagement in campus and community activities. The learning community was piloted in Fall 2014 and included a transfer student seminar (co-taught by an FYTS faculty member and an OTP staff member) that was linked with a psychology course. The foundation of the learning community was influenced by the positive psychology literature and research on flourishing (Seligman, 2011), as well as the three elements of self-authorship: trusting the internal voice, building an internal foundation, and securing internal commitments (Baxter Magolda, 2008). Activities and assignments in the learning community included a student engagement plan and culminating portfolio assignment, and were designed with consideration to the elements of self-authorship with the goal of fostering self-authorship development in the transfer student participants. Students in the transfer learning community ranged in age, number of credits transferred to the institution, and academic preparation/background. The type of institution from which the students transferred also varied greatly among the students in the class—some transferred from "feeder" two-year institutions—while others transferred from smaller or even comparable four-year universities. Students were invited to participate in the learning community during summer orientation and through personalized email messages.

PROGRAM DESCRIPTION

Transfer students are a growing population on college and university campuses (Hossler et al., 2012). The National Center for Education Statistics (NCES, 2008) estimated that one in five new students at four-year institutions have transferred from another college or university. Growth in the number of transfer students, and in the types of unique transitional experiences of these students, was the impetus for engaging in a self-study process of the programs, processes, and procedures that affect transfer student success at KSU. The university has offered a variety of institutional initiatives, including first-year seminars, learning communities, orientation programs, and peer mentoring programs to help students transition into college. But most efforts were aimed at supporting first-year students. The development of the transfer seminar was in response to the findings of the Foundations of Excellence® (FoE) Transfer Focus self-study conducted at KSU, and informed by the FoE Steering Committee. One of the recommendations in the study was to create targeted programs, including a transfer student seminar (Kennesaw State University, 2013). The rationale for creating new curricular and co-curricular programs was to engage transfer students with faculty, staff, and peers, with the aim of improving transfer student retention, progression, and graduation (Foote, Kranzow, & Hinkle, 2015). With more than half of the new students entering as transfers, KSU's Campus Completion Plan for the Complete College Georgia Initiative recognized the need to provide a supportive and engaging environment for this specific population.

The content and approach to teaching the transfer student seminar took into consideration the findings and recommendations from the FoE study (qualitative data from student, faculty, and staff surveys) as well as the action steps described in KSU's Completion Plan. As the FoE final report indicates, "existing research on transfer students suggests that an effective success strategy often involves the creation of dedicated programs as well as the deliberate and timely engagement of new transfer students into existing structures" (Kennesaw State University, 2013, p. 2). The transfer student seminar and learning community responded to the need for dedicated transfer programs, and to the importance of engaging these students into the KSU campus culture.

In Fall 2013, a 2-credit hour, 10-week, transfer student seminar was piloted under KSU 2290, an FYTS special topics course designator. The course was offered again in Spring 2014 before it was revised and included in the "Flourishing at KSU" transfer student learning community in Fall 2014. Prior to launching the learning community, a common reader, *The Power of Habit* (Duhigg, 2012), was selected as a supplemental text (in addition to a customized textbook authored by FYTS faculty), and the course was revised to include information and assignments that integrated aspects of positive psychology, specifically around the ideas of flourishing, hope, and resilience, and self-authorship development. Self-authorship, "the internal capacity to define one's beliefs, identity, and social relations" (Baxter Magolda, 2008, p. 269), was selected as a theoretical framework for the seminar because of its relevance to the transfer transition, and the relationship of the elements of self-authorship (trusting the internal voice, building an internal foundation, and securing internal commitments, Baxter Magolda, 2008) to the individual experiences of transfer students.

To facilitate the process of self-authorship development and flourishing, a student in the learning community completes a Student Engagement Plan (SEP)[1] within the first week of classes in the fall. The five-part SEP begins with a personal reflection and identification of a personal challenge (related to academic skill development, personal health and wellness, involvement, service, academic motivation, learning a new skill or hobby, and leadership development). This personal challenge becomes the focus of the goal-setting part of the plan. After learning about campus resources and opportunities, a student creates a plan for engagement that reflects the personal challenge they identified in the first part of the SEP. As a student develops their plans for engagement, they identify potential obstacles and strategies, or resources to overcome the potential obstacles. This part of the SEP was focused on guiding a student through the process of developing personal resiliency, a struggle for some because of past experiences. To communicate the utility of all of the parts of the SEP, the culminating section of the plan requires a student to reflect and articulate, through a mind-mapping exercise, the relationship between their academic and co-curricular experiences and their personal goals.

---

1   Adapted from Office of Student Engagement and Success Center at the University of South Carolina

During the semester, students were asked periodically to revisit their SEP through a series of smaller assignments that helped connect course content to the information, ideas, and goals described in the SEP assignment. For example, one of the initial assignments asked students to identify who they are as learners and to reflect on their academic and personal experiences and how these experiences impacted their academic identity development. The habit loop from *The Power of Habit* (Duhigg, 2012), was presented to guide students in the process of developing or revising existing study and/or other habits connected to their personal challenges. Students also completed the StrengthsQuest and learned how to use the results of that assessment to approach challenging academic or personal situations. The StrengthsQuest results were also used to help students make meaning of previous experiences and determine how they might use that new knowledge moving forward (part of the self-authorship journey). Personal strengths and self-authorship were also referenced as students developed "Elevator Speeches" that could be used to make a personal "pitch" to someone in 60-90 seconds.

In addition to engaging students in personal reflection and application of the skills, information, and new knowledge learned through the readings and discussions in the classroom, students also had several assignments and activities that took them out of the classroom to become engaged in the university. For example, "Campus Event Selfies" was an assignment that involved attending a campus or university-sponsored event and taking a picture (selfie) to document participation in the event. A team photo scavenger hunt was also completed during part of one class meeting and then presented during the second half of the class meeting. This assignment motivated students to work collaboratively to locate various campus resources and the services offered. The presentation of team photos helped students who had not visited the service(s) to become familiar with resources and locations, which the students believed would increase the likelihood that they would visit that office or department at a later time.

The culminating transfer student seminar assignment was a portfolio with the following components: 1) A personal plan of study connected with an academic major, and personal career exploration and/or goals; 2) Documentation of participation in undergraduate research, community service, or campus activities; 3) An interview with a professional or academic mentor; and 4) A personal reflection. The final reflection required students to respond to questions that connected aspects of the class to their learning and engagement while continuing to foster self-authorship development and flourishing. Specifically, students were asked to discuss the relationship between participation in the course and the transfer student learning community, the extent to which this relationship influenced perceptions of academic identity ("Who am I as a student or learner?"), then to reflect on the ways in which engagement in the seminar contributed to their perceptions about their ability to be successful at the university and accomplish academic or personal goals. Student reflections demonstrated the extent to which their perceptions about themselves, particularly who they were as students, and engagement had transformed. For many students, they had changed majors and/or career aspirations during the semester, which they attributed to the information and assignments in the class. Both in the reflections and in the presentation of the portfolios, students discussed newfound confidence related to their personal challenges and goals.

After the course ended, students were invited to participate in one-on-one interviews focused on perceptions of self-authorship development associated with participation in the transfer student learning community.[2] The interview protocol was informed by questions included in the Reflective Conversation Guide (Baxter Magolda & King, 2008) and the Self-Authorship Survey. Interview questions asked student participants to reflect on the relationship between perceptions of KSU and actual experiences at the university and in the learning community, and the influence of these experiences on academic and personal goals. The data from the interviews indicated that students with willingness to confront difficult decisions and self-author that process had a clearer vision of their academic and professional goals with a measurable and detailed plan of action. For example, one student described how participation in the transfer student seminar helped him look critically at his decision to return to college after a long absence:

> [It] forced me to more closely analyze my plans for going back to college as an adult, especially with regards [sic] to my goal of getting a degree beyond the four-year degree. It was Maslow's hierarchy that really helped clarify things for me, strangely enough. Getting a Master's of Science in Library Science and working at a university doesn't mean I give up on my other educational goals, and on attaining self-actualization and, ultimately, transcendence. In fact, it is a necessary step to get there from here. I'm really looking forward to it in a way I hadn't expected before taking KSU 2290.

Another student discussed her decision to change her major following a class session focused on "Everything I Wished I Had Known about Advising as a Transfer Student," with a presentation from the Director of Advising for New, Exploratory, and Students in Transition (NEST) at KSU. He shared his personal reflections and advice from the perspective of an

2   Pilot research study funded by NODA and NASPA Region III

advisor and former transfer student at KSU. After the presentation in class, the student reflected on her lifelong goal of becoming a nurse and shared the following:

> I've actually begun thinking about changing my major from Nursing to Early Childhood Education, which is surprising because I came to KSU for the Nursing program. I realized in the class that I did not see myself as a nurse. It was a big deal for me because although I had considered teaching, I always returned to nursing. It was Dr. XX's talk in our class that influenced my final decision. I emailed him and we set up an appointment to talk about my major change. I feel like I finally have a plan for my future.

The outcomes were very different for other student participants. For example, a few participants described making decisions that affirmed habits that had negative results or consequences (i.e., choosing to withdraw from a class or classes rather than seeking help or meeting with an advisor to discuss a change of major; hanging out with friends rather than attending classes). Student participants who showed evidence of self-authorship in the one-on-one interviews were more likely to change personal habits to align with their goals. Specifically, students reported changing habits related to the use of social media (one student discussed deleting her Facebook page because she recognized she was spending significant amounts of time connecting with "old" friends), partying and/or socializing, and choosing to do things that were familiar and/or comfortable.

Finally, student reflections and interview data demonstrated limited intersections between the transfer student seminar and psychology course embedded in the learning community. Attempts at creating integrative assignments and activities between the courses were unsuccessful because approximately a third of the students in the transfer student learning community were not enrolled in both courses. Because the learning community was offered as a pilot in Fall 2014, a decision was made to allow students who did not need the psychology course–perhaps because they had satisfied that with a course transferred from their previous institution–to enroll in the transfer student seminar as a standalone course.

END RESULT AND IMPACT, LESSONS LEARNED

Despite many positive outcomes associated with the pilot implementation of the "Flourishing at KSU" transfer student learning community, several changes were made to prepare to offer the learning community on a larger scale. The learning outcomes for the transfer student seminar were revised to focus more explicitly on personal planning, academic exploration, and engagement (Table 6.1).

Table 6.1
Transfer Student Seminar Revised Student Learning Outcomes

Students will:	Develop a personal plan of study connected with an academic major and personal career exploration and/or goals.
	Engage in academic exploration and provide relevant examples demonstrating the relationship between the new knowledge gained through that process to current or future actions and/or learning in a discipline or area of study.
	Apply academic strategies, including goal-setting, time management, and study strategies.
	Identify and engage in experiences outside of the classroom to foster connection to the institution and development of personal identity as a student.

The new learning outcomes for the course were used to revise the existing seminar portfolio rubric, which was adapted to measure the stated outcomes in the transfer student seminar and in similar seminars at the University of Tennessee-Knoxville (UTK) and the University of North Carolina Wilmington (UNCW) (Appendix A). The portfolio rubric, along with a demographic survey, will also be used in a multi-campus study at KSU, UTK, and UNCW to determine the extent to which participation in a transfer student seminar influences students' perceptions of development in academic and career exploration, planning, and engagement.[3]

In addition to revising the course-level student learning outcomes and portfolio rubric for the transfer student seminar, the "Flourishing at KSU" learning community was modified to link the seminar with *WELL 1000: Foundations for Healthy Living*, a general education course and a requirement that most incoming students do not satisfy at the point of transfer. The SEP and culminating portfolio assignment will be integrated throughout the learning community classes to ensure that the themes and ideas extend beyond the transfer student seminar. In Spring 2015, the transfer student seminar was reviewed and approved at KSU and will now

---

3   Foote, S. M., Curtis, R. T., & Mastrogiovanni, J. (2015). *A multi-campus study to measure perceptions of academic exploration and engagement measured by a common rubric in a transfer student seminar.* Catalyst grant funded by NODA.

be offered under a permanent course designator beginning in Fall 2015. The "Flourishing at KSU" learning community is conceived as a cornerstone of KSU's new Transfer Advocacy Gateway (TAG) program that will be offered to underserved transfers from two-year colleges beginning in 2015.[4] The TAG program will also include support from dedicated enrollment service specialists to work with students before they transfer to KSU, graduation coaches that serve as a point-of-contact and provide support to TAG students until the students graduate, and a variety of workshops focused on fostering academic and personal success.[5]

RECOMMENDATIONS AND LIMITATIONS

The pilot offering of the "Flourishing at KSU" transfer student learning community achieved many of the intended outcomes; however, the impact was limited because not all students were enrolled in both courses in the learning community. Additionally, because transfer students were not required to take a transfer student seminar, recruiting students to participate in the learning community presented several challenges. Identifying specific populations of transfer students–particularly those who transfer before earning an associate's degree–might result in higher interest and a potentially larger learning community enrollment. With the implementation of the TAG program at KSU, there will be a dedicated group of students in the program who will participate in the learning community. Furthermore, revising the student learning outcomes in the transfer student seminar and intentionally linking that course with WELL 1000 will make the learning community potentially more effective and appealing to many transfer students. Finally, continuing to collect data, from the course and from research embedded in the learning community, will provide an opportunity for continuous revision and improvement to the "Flourishing at KSU" learning community.

As the university scales the transfer student learning community offerings in tandem with the launch of the TAG program, there are additional efforts aimed at improving the success of transfer students underway. For example, there is a campus-wide Transfer Advisory Council and ongoing discussion of creating a required online orientation for transfer students (the current transfer student orientation is optional). A transfer peer mentoring program and other variations of the transfer student learning

4   Wade-Berg, J., Rascati, R. J., & Foote, S. M. (2014). *Strengthening bridges for student success: Increasing transfer and completion rates for underrepresented, underprepared, and low-income community and technical college students seeking four-year degrees*. Grant proposal funded by the Fund for the Improvement of Postsecondary Education (FIPSE)—First in the World Program (FITW).
5   Additional information about the TAG program is available: http://www.academicimpressions.com/news/spotlight-innovation-how-kennesaws-tag-program-creating-better-degree-completion-pathways

community are in development, and in the fall a community that links the transfer student seminar to a chemistry course will be piloted.

Cost of the Initiative and Source of Funding

The transfer student learning community was implemented without any dedicated funding, and the instructors taught the courses as part of their teaching load. While no funding was needed to develop and pilot the learning community, external funding from NODA and NASPA Region III helped support research on the perceived impact of participation in the transfer student learning community. Additional external funding from the FITW FIPSE grant will allow the learning community to be offered annually to approximately 200 students in the TAG program.

References

Baxter Magolda, M. B. (2008). Three elements of self-authorship. *Journal of College Student Development, 49*(4), 269-284.

Baxter Magolda, M. B., & King, P. M. (2008). *Toward reflective conversations: An advising approach that promotes self-authorship. Peer Review, 10*(1), 8-11.

Duhigg, C. (2012). *The power of habit: Why we do what we do in life and business.* New York, NY: Random House.

Foote, S. M., Kranzow, J., Hinkle, S. (2015). *Focusing on the forgotten: An examination of the influences and innovative practices that affect community college transfer student success.* In S. J. Jones and D. L. Jackson (Eds.) *Examining the Impact of Community Colleges on the Global Workforce.*

Hossler, D., Shapiro, D., Dundar, A., Ziskin, M., Chen, J., Zerquera, D., & Torres, V. (2012). *Transfer & mobility: A National view of pre-degree student movement in postsecondary institutions* [Signature Report 2]. Retrieved from http://nscresearchcenter.org/wp-content/uploads/NSC_Signature_Report_2.pdf

Kennesaw State University (2013). *Transforming the transfer experience: Findings and recommendations from the KSU Foundations of Excellence transfer self-study process.* Unpublished report.

National Center for Educational Statistics (2008). *Descriptive summary of 2003-04 beginning postsecondary students: Three years later* (NCES Report 2008-174). Washington, DC: US Department of Education. Retrieved from http://nces.ed.gov/Pubsearch/pubsinfo.asp?pubid=2008174

Seligman, M. E. P. (2011). *Flourish.* New York, NY: Free Press.

INSTITUTIONAL DESCRIPTION

Name and Location:
Kennesaw State University (KSU), Northwest Georgia

Institution Type:
Comprehensive, four-year university

Institutional Selectivity:
Moderately selective

Size of Enrollment:
Approximately 32,500 students in more than 100 undergraduate and graduate programs (master's and doctoral-level) across two campuses. During the academic years 2005-2014, the number of transfer students entering KSU each fall outnumbered the number of incoming first-year students.

APPENDIX A: TRANSFER PORTFOLIO RUBRIC

Purpose

The purpose of this rubric is to determine the extent to which participating in a transfer seminar at UNCW, UT-Knoxville, and Kennesaw State University promotes development (or students' perceptions of development) in the major areas evaluated by the rubric.

Common Portfolio Content and Areas of Evaluation

1. **Personal Planning**: This section accounts for the development of a personal plan comprised of a major/career plan, and/or an academic plan.
2. **Academic Exploration**: In this section, students will describe interactions with a faculty member, academic advisor, or academic mentor and the extent to which those interactions have contributed to the academic development and exploration of the student. Additionally, students will also reflect on the integration of new academic knowledge into their development as a student.
3. **Engagement**: Students will describe how experiential learning and engagement outside of the formal classroom contribute to their connection to the institution, personal development and transition, and identity as a student.

Category	Excellent	Satisfactory	Needs Improvement	Incomplete or Not Achieved
Personal Planning	Identifies a focused, realistic personal plan of study that accounts for all remaining coursework, plans for internship(s), and career	Identifies a focused, realistic personal plan of study that accounts for most of the remaining coursework, plans for internship(s), and career	Personal plan may not be realistic or it may fail to address any of the areas described in the "Excellent" category	Information is missing or incomplete
Academic Exploration	Makes explicit references to interactions or engagement with faculty, academic mentors, or advisors. Describes the extent to which those interactions facilitated or will facilitate the process of academic exploration. Explains through several examples how the student will use or is using what he or she has learned and application of knowledge to current or future actions and/or learning in his or her discipline/area of study	Provides some reference to interactions with a faculty member, academic mentor, or advisor. Describes, with limited detail, how those interactions might facilitate academic exploration, and how the student might use his or her new knowledge in future	Information is not present or fails to address any of the elements in the "Excellent" category	Information is missing or incomplete
Engagement	Provides multiple examples that demonstrate meaningful connections among experiences outside of the classroom to foster connection to the institution and development of personal identity as a student	Provides limited examples that demonstrate meaningful connections among experiences outside of the classroom to foster connection to the institution and development of personal identity as a student	Information is not present or fails to address any of the elements in the "Excellent" category	Information is missing or incomplete

Stephanie M. Foote *is a professor of education and the director of the Master of Science in First-Year Studies at Kennesaw State University.*

C. Jean So *is an instructor of education and the assistant director of the office of orientation and transition programs at Kennesaw State University.*

7

THE TRANSFER ACADEMY FOR
TOMORROW'S ENGINEERS (TATE)

Carmen Fies and Joseph Kulhanek

INSTITUTIONAL DESCRIPTION

The University of Texas at San Antonio (UTSA) is a selective, doctoral-granting public institution, with an undergraduate enrollment of 22,305.

STATEMENT OF THE ISSUE

The persistent shortfall of students choosing a STEM field for their future careers, especially engineering, is exacerbated by the continued underrepresentation of minorities and women in these fields (National Research Council, 2012). The 2007 CSRC Research Report (Rivas, Perez, Alvarez, & Solorzano, 2007) on Latina/o transfer students presents a careful investigation of one of the more 'porous' components of the educational pipeline: transfer from two- to four-year institutions. The program described here is located in an area that includes significant numbers of underrepresented students (for example, 63.2% of the local population is Hispanic) and where only 24.2% earned a bachelor's degree or higher (U.S. Census Bureau, 2014).

SHORT OVERVIEW

To help address the underrepresentation of ethnic minority students and women in engineering, the Transfer Academy for Tomorrow's Engineers (TATE) program was developed by a team of administrators and faculty representing regional two- and four-year postsecondary institutions. This program supports student transfer from a community college to a four-year institution as they pursue a bachelor's degree in engineering. The specific focus of TATE was designed in response to needs voiced by members of the local engineering community to improve students' technical writing, as well as their presentation and group work skills.

TATE consists of two major components: 1) an intensive Summer Bridging Institute (SBI); and 2) a "community of practice" that includes faculty, staff, and peer mentors. The TATE-SBI is organized around climate research, a topic designed not only to challenge students to engage in traditional learning activities, but to also create educational videos. Civil Engineering and Writing Program faculty facilitate the instruction and student activities.

Across the three years we report on here, TATE-SBI has welcomed sixty-three transfer students. Forty-seven of these students (74.6%) transferred to the participating four-year institution. Of those students, thirty-six (76.6%) remain engineering majors, five are enrolled in a new major, four are in good standing and still engineering majors, but not currently enrolled, and one of the students already graduated (see Table 7.1).

Table 7.1

TATE Student Enrollments: 2012-2014

Year & Cohort	TATE-SBI Enrollment	Transfer to UTSA, College of Engineering (CoE)	Enrolled in UTSA, CoE (March 2015)	Enrolled, but in a new major
2012 – I	20	18	11	5
2013 – II	29	18	14	
2014 – III	14	11	11	
Totals	**63**	**47**	**36**	**5**

PROGRAM DESCRIPTION

The TATE program is a collaborative partnership designed to increase the academic success of individuals who might not otherwise have access to postsecondary training in engineering, including underrepresented ethnic minority students, women, and students who are the first in their family to attend college. As of March 2015, the program has served three cohorts of students and is in the process of reaching out to students for the 2015 cycle. The total of sixty-three students who participated in the first three years of the TATE Summer experience were recruited from seven community colleges.

The balance of this paper describes the inter- and intra-institutional coordination process that led to the TATE program, followed by a description of educational and academic outcomes across the three years of its existence.

Coordination Process

At a gathering of local university and industry leaders, employers revealed that they were reluctant to hire local graduates because they lacked appropriate skills in technical writing, interpersonal communication, and presentation abilities, all skills needed to excel in engineering. In an effort to remedy these shortfalls, higher education leaders from the local two- and four-year institutions agreed to jointly develop a transfer model for engineering students. The partners develop a set of articulation agreements and a Memorandum of Understanding (MoU), which led to the establishment the TATE program in 2012. In addition, the four-year institution identified scholarship resources to aid in the recruitment of students. A team of instructors and administrators from all participating institutions developed the curriculum and instructional sequence for the TATE-SBI.

Recruitment in the first year took place exclusively at the local community colleges, but broadened in years 2 and 3 to include community colleges in the larger region. In the first year (2012), students selected for the program needed to major in engineering, possess a minimum transfer GPA of 2.25, and be the first in their family to attend a four-year college. After the first year, the GPA minimum was raised to 2.80.

Recruiting students in the first year was challenging because the program was new and the timespan between the program's approval and the beginning of the summer session was short. This led to the acceptance of students who did not meet the selection criteria, but who were recommended by community college faculty. Student recruitment was more successful in the following years because the program was better known and had a successful track record.

The number of students who could be accommodated has varied from year-to-year due to funding. In the first year, all participants received financial support, regardless of their academic performance in the TATE-SBI. In the second year, however, the program required that students successfully complete the TATE-SBI by actively participating in all aspects of the summer program, including attendance at orientation meetings, lectures, workshops, fieldtrips, tutoring sessions, and independent group study sessions. The culminating outcome of the summer session consisted of a research presentation with panel feedback, and creation of an associated webcast. Please visit the following link for an example of a webcast titled: Global Climate Change from Land Cover (https://www.youtube.com/watch?v=4TwB3Bb-RWU).

One of the main goals of the program is to attract the participation of students from underrepresented groups, including ethnic minority students, females, and students who were first in their family to attend college. As the following Table 7.2 shows, most participants are members of a targeted minority group. However, the first three years of the program resulted in only nine female participants.

Table 7.2

TATE Student Characteristics by Cohort

Year & Cohort	Latin@	White/ Caucasian	Asian/ Asian American	Black/ African American	Native American/ Native Alaskan
2012 – I	10	7	0	1	0
2013 – II	13	3	1	1	0
2014 – III	4	1	3	1	2
Totals	**27**	**11**	**4**	**3**	**2**

Summer Program Outcomes

Across the six weeks of the TATE-SBI, participants spend most mornings of the first two weeks in class, followed by group meetings. Students also participate in field trips, providing them with an opportunity to explore applied engineering work. In weeks three through five, activities shift to a faculty-facilitated intensive writing experience that is structured around small groups, each addressing a different global climate-oriented research topic. At the end of week six, students present their research results along with a video webcast that connects the topic to local engineering challenges to a panel of reviewers.

At the end of each summer program, participants who successfully complete the TATE-SBI are invited to apply for a $6,000 scholarship at the four-year institution. The scholarship is offered on a competitive basis and students submit an application that includes an essay section.

The instructional core team consists of faculty members at the four-year institution; one is a faculty member in the College of Engineering and the other is part of the institution's writing program. The members of the instructional core team design and implement all learning events. They also accompany students on field trips.

Student Perceptions

At the end of each cohort's summer experience, students are asked to complete surveys focused on three specific competencies: writing, presenting, and working in teams. Results include the following:

- *Writing Skills*: Across all cohorts students ranked the writing component highly. Participants overwhelmingly reported that they felt more confident and proficient in their ability to produce technical writing. However, the instructional team revised assignments after the first year. This revision was in direct response to comments by Cohort I participants' indicating that some of their writing tasks were not clearly linked to engineering topics. Cohorts II and III rated the revised writing tasks as helpful and appropriate.

- *Presentation Skills:* Participants in each cohort presented their projects at the end of the TATE-SBI, however, the forum in which they made their presentations changed every year in response to student feedback. Cohort I students presented their work to a panel of local experts. Cohort II students presented their findings to a smaller, but still public forum. Cohort III students presented only to the participants of the TATE-SBI, without an external panel of reviewers. Revisions to the presentation strategy changed initially because Cohort I participants perceived their experience as high stakes and high pressure. This feedback led to the redesign of the final presentation, which included UTSA faculty members only. Cohort III participants made presentations to their instructors and peers only.

- *Teamwork Skills:* Each of the cohorts was asked to rate the degree to which teamwork had a positive impact on their TATE-SBI experience. Mean ratings for each cohort increased each year (5 ="highly successful"): Cohort I = 3.6, Cohort II = 4.07, and Cohort II − 4.12.

Student and Instructor Perception

Perceptions of the program's effectiveness vary between instructors and students. For example, although the instructional team considered the presentations by guest speakers as highly effective, students attending the same sessions were less impressed. In addition, the students considered the balance between lectures and hands-on opportunities as less ideal than the faculty members.

Mentoring after the TATE-SBI

Upon acceptance into an engineering undergraduate program at the four-year institution, the TATE facilitator invites students to participate in monthly meetings that take place during the fall and spring semesters. These meetings, which are open to members of all TATE cohorts, help students to support one another academically through a peer network called the Student Learning Community (TATE-SLC). In this community, participants gain insight about different engineering programs, study skills, career services, time management, internships, research opportunities, faculty lectures and many other topics designed to help students succeed in their transition into UTSA. Aside from face-to-face support from TATE facilitators and the peer groups, students receive monthly newsletters outlining additional opportunities to stay involved.

End Result and Impact/Lessons Learned

Based on student feedback, the following strategies are under consideration for future cohorts:

- Integrate hands-on whole-group and small-group explorations, as well as field trips that concretize abstract concepts.
- Revise time frames for specific tasks (e.g., ensure participants have video footage to work with before the session on video creation takes place).
- Create an explicit statement of what is expected of participants during the recruitment phase.
- Link financial support to successful completion of all aspects of the summer program, including consistent attendance.

Instruction

The quality of student engagement was influenced positively when students met with instructors outside of mandatory sessions. This, in turn, helped instructors make better use of scheduled classroom time. Instructors also narrowed the range of topics to be discussed in subsequent cohorts, which provided students with more in-depth understanding. For example, instructor's modeling of an in-depth analysis of a research paper significantly improved the student outcomes as well as time spent on task.

Activities and Experiences

Students emphasized the value of the program's field trip experiences as a way to connect new learning with real world contexts, including insights into how human activity impacts the environment. Further, participants highly valued networking opportunities, and noted how networking with faculty and peers alike was beneficial for their development.

Skill Development

Students indicated that mathematical preparation was critical for success in this program. They also gained increased confidence in writing throughout the summer experience, including their ability to write technical reports. Further, they indicated that the hands-on experience of finding reliable research publications were of substantive value. It should also be noted that each cohort benefited significantly from the required group presentations. Instructors noted that most transfer students did not have extensive experience preparing and delivering PowerPoint presentations. The need to provide additional support in this area was suggested to the community college partners.

Peer Mentoring and Recruitment

The P-20 Director who is currently responsible for facilitating the SBI has identified students from each cohort who were willing to mentor incoming students. The TATE students have a space on campus that allows them to interact with other students who are supported through P-20 programming, such as the McNair Scholars, Louis Stokes Alliance for Minority Participation (LSAMP), and the Collegiate G-Force Work-Study Mentorships. Students receive both academic and social support and have a "safe space" to ask questions and relax. In addition to mentoring, students from each cohort may assist with the recruitment process by visiting their former campuses. As a result, the selection process for the 2015 cohort has been more effective as a result of students sharing their personal experiences. Examples of personal testimonials can be found in video link titled: *UTSA TATE* https://www.youtube.com/watch?v=Z5BA2u88Mj8

Recommendations and Limitations

The six-week summer session has worked well to address the overall objectives of the program. The team indicated that they enjoyed working together and were pleased with the available organizational support supplied by Blackboard Learn. In particular, having students' IDs already established through the Registrar's Office facilitated communication and resource sharing.

The major strategy missing from the 2014 cohort was a panel of reviewers for students' end-of-program presentations. It is believed that panel feedback is especially important for student development and consideration is being given to the implementation of a new panel for future cohorts.

A second change impacts students' stipend payments. Future stipends will be linked to students' program performance. Cohort I-III participants received a stipend for attending the SBI, even though many of the students did not complete all of the tasks. In an effort to provide additional motivation for program completion, Cohort IV participants will receive scholarships based on the degree to which they complete all tasks.

Although the program achieved success in recruiting students from ethnic minority backgrounds, increasing the participation of women was less successful. At the time of this writing, however, a Latina who participated in Cohort I will graduate with a B.S. in Engineering and another will graduate later this year. In addition, it is hoped that enhanced outreach to regional colleges will increase the number of female participants who are interested in becoming engineers. TATE recruitment initiatives have taken place at the Alamo Colleges, Del Mar College, Laredo Community College and Lone Star College.

As a result of lessons learned over the three-year period, the next scheduled iteration of the 2016 TATE-SBI will include two major changes. First, participating institutions will be asked to cover the instructional costs involved with delivery of the curriculum. Second, instead of stipends, a scholarship model will be implemented. At the end of the program, the students will receive a scholarship that is determined by student's individual effort, and is applicable only to studies in one of the undergraduate engineering programs at UTSA.

Finally, the university is expanding the model to include a chemistry cohort for the summer of 2016. The intent is to provide the faculty from Alamo Colleges and the UTSA College of Science with an opportunity to determine if the SBI model will be effective for other disciplines. Alignment meetings have taken place between faculty and staff from both institutions. A thorough review of degree plans is taking place with the hope to identify instructional needs and improve advising for interested students.

Cost of the Initiative, Source of Funding

The major program costs included faculty time, student stipends, food, parking, and the first year field trip. All subsequent trips were local and free.

The program received support from the following sources:

- "Climate Change Communication: Engineering, Environmental Science, and Education," Sponsored by NASA, $643,243.00 (2011 to Present). A portion of the amount was allocated to support the instruction, field trips, and stipends.

- The program received funding from both the Long and Pioneer Foundations. The monies were used to provide scholarships to the incoming TATE students.
- Institutional support was provided by the UTSA Office of P-20 Initiatives.

REFERENCES

Kulhanek, J., & Fies, C. (2014). *Transfer Academy for Tomorrow's Engineers (TATE)*. Atlanta, GA.

National Research Council. (2012). *Research Universities and the Future of America: Ten Breakthrough Actions Vital to Our Nation's Prosperity and Security*. Washington, DC: National Academies Press.

Rivas, M. A., Perez, J., Alvarez, C. R., & Solorzano, D. G. (2007). Latina/o Transfer Students: Understanding the Critical Role of the Transfer Process in California's Postsecondary Institutions. (CSRC Research Report. Number 9 ed.). Los Angeles: UCLA Chicano Studies Research Center.

U.S. Census Bureau. (2014). State and County QuickFacts. Data derived from Population Estimates, American Community Survey, Census of Population and Housing, County Business Patterns, Economic Census, Survey of Business Owners, Building Permits, Census of Governments. Retrieved November 11, 2014

Carmen Fies *is an associate professor of STEM education & instructional technology, and an associate professor of chemistry education at the University of Texas at San Antonio.*

Joseph Kulhanek *is the assistant vice president for the office of P-20 initiatives at the University of Texas at San Antonio.*

8

Transfer Star Stories

Adam D. Joncich and Joshua Henderson

Statement of the Issue

In college it is widely assumed that a student will begin at age 18, attend for four years, develop personal and professional identities, take classes, join a club or two, get an internship, and graduate. This dominant story, however, is not applicable to transfer students, who constitute an increasingly large proportion of the college-going population. Transfer Star Stories was designed not only to provide artistic communications and performance training to NYC transfer students, but also to describe the rich dimensions of the transfer student experience, highlight the value these students bring to any college community, and advocate for the needs of transfer students overall.

Overview

Transfer students represent a significant and growing sector on college campuses, at both 2- and 4-year institutions. It is estimated that one-third of all students transfer at least once in college, and up to a quarter will transfer multiple times (Marling, 2013). Given that high school graduation rates are anticipated to decrease by 3% between now and 2020, experts anticipate that four-year institutions will seek to recruit more transfer students from two-year community colleges to fill seats that would otherwise be filled by first-time college students (Handel, 2013). Yet transfer students are often left to "fend for themselves" and "figure out" on their own often complex academic transitions (Tobolowsky & Cox, 2012). The result is that while more students are transferring and populating college classrooms, they remain largely invisible in terms of programming and support. These circumstances highlight the urgency to facilitate and improve both the transfer experience and educational development practices for transfer students.

To this end, recent research has shown that the sharing of student stories is associated with academic success for vulnerable populations (Walton & Cohen, 2011). This project was designed to foster the development and dissemination of transfer student stories on a college campus through the implementation of "Transfer Star Stories." Results from this grant-funded, 12-week storytelling initiative illuminates the transfer student experience through the use of a unique performance-centered strategy.

PROGRAM DESCRIPTION

Background

This project was designed to create a fine arts performance program, which provided "mindfulness-based" storytelling training to a group of transfer students from New York City. Mindfulness is a concept and practice considered essential to human functioning, and is originally rooted in ancient Eastern religious tradition (Brown & Ryan, 2003). The study of mindfulness has blossomed in many areas of Western science and has recently garnered attention in higher education research. For example, studies show evidence that practice in mindfulness can improve mental functioning as it relates to classwork (Bush, 2011). It is also associated with enhanced academic achievement among transfer students (Joncich, 2013).

In addition to mindfulness, storytelling is similarly important as a means for humans to express themselves (Fisher, 1987). Telling stories about our lives is a timeless and universal means by which human beings understand the world and their roles within it. In some higher educational contexts, storytelling has been shown to be vital in effective advisement (Hagen, 2007), and in fostering student connection, expression, classroom engagement, and critical thinking skills (MacDrury & Alterio, 2003). This initiative applies storytelling as a means to introduce to a group of transfers an art form that fosters expression and growth through mindful sharing of educational and cultural experience.

Objectives

The aims of the program were to: 1) develop storytelling training as a cohort-building experience and highlight storytelling as a trainable skill for transfer students; 2) produce videos of transfer students' educational stories for college use; and 3) increase awareness of transfer student experiences and stories through cultural exchange and performance art.

Recruitment

Students were nominated for participation by faculty and staff at the college. Students were required to have transferred into the school but there were no specific achievement requirements. Most of the 10 participants were high performing students who had been in the school for one or more semesters at the time of training.

Training Exercises

The program was designed and executed in partnership with Narativ Inc., an organization with experience in storytelling training. Sessions were held once a week for twelve weeks off campus at an arts training facility in Manhattan. Training occurred for two hours from 6:30 to 8:30 pm in consecutive weeks with one week off in the middle of the semester due to midterms. Students were provided with funds for transportation, if needed.

Each two-hour session was split into two separate one-hour sub-lessons. The first hour focused on didactic learning and the second on storytelling technique. During the first half of the session, topics related to storytelling and communication skills were covered. Exercises focused on story mapping, pacing, annunciation, stage presence, movement and detailed description. The second half of each class featured communal storytelling with prompts targeting themes such as transition, perseverance, and community building. Participants sat in a circle and took turns applying storytelling and listening skills. Video of the training sequences was collected at the beginning, middle, and end of the training period.

Performance Execution

The culminating performance took place at the Abingdon Theater, an Off Broadway 98-seat theater in midtown Manhattan. Promotional materials, such as flyers and posters, were distributed on campus. Electronic advertisements were distributed to the public. The audience featured a mix of family, students, public, and friends of performers. Participants were asked to arrive at the theater for warm ups; they were provided dinner, and the performance started at 8:10 pm. Each participant performed his/her story, and the show ended at around 9:45 pm. A video of each student story performance (about 6 minutes per story) was produced and distributed to each participant.

Program Assessment

In addition to the 10 students who participated, a graduate student employee of the program was also present in each training session. The purpose of his participation was to gain first-hand experience with the program and assess the effectiveness of the activities. This individual then conducted assessment interviews. In addition, videos, surveys, and interviews executed by Narativ were made available for reporting. Subjective reports gleaned from these interviews are presented below, highlighting the development of skills and reported experiences of improvements in areas such as confidence, self-reflection, and wellness.

END RESULTS AND LESSONS LEARNED

This program demonstrated that transfer students have important stories to share and that their articulation of these stories may help transfers to develop self-confidence, communication skills, and a sense of community.

Students were engaged in this program from start to finish. The ten students who were originally selected for the program completed all elements of the training, with a 93 percent attendance record. This degree of participation was remarkable, as training occurred off campus.

The stated objectives of the program were achieved, which included the implementation and assessment of a twelve-week program that helped college transfer students learn to tell stories, listen to each other, and communicate more effectively and artistically. This approach has subsequently been presented to larger student audiences, as well as to faculty and staff.

Interview Results

Student participants were asked to address two questions about their role in Transfer Star Stories and the impact this activity had on them. The following quotes highlight some of the main insights gleaned from the participants:

1. What skills did you learned from this program?

> I learned to pay attention to my surroundings when I'm telling a story, like you have to recreate it. The room, the people, the smells—these are all subtle things that you really don't notice, till someone says like 'hey, have you ever thought about what did that room look like?' How were you feeling, were you shaking, were your hands sweating?' It's taught me how to come across more clearly, even just when explaining how was my day.

> Being in a safe space with people from different backgrounds where we didn't know each other allowed me to see the world from another perspective and to see others' background. Be able to accept other people's background and they accept mine. Communication helped me to do that.

Acknowledging the obstacles you have every day, whatever's getting in the way of your listening, if you don't acknowledge that first then it's going to keep being in your listening throughout the whole program.

I cried my first time in class, and just to have that level of comfort and openness and people to genuinely listen to me because I didn't notice how valuable the power of listening was till this class. It's made me more aware of my surroundings, like, the friends I have, do they really even listen to me?

2. How and under what circumstances do you see yourself applying these skills in the future?

    I could walk into any interview and be very articulate when responding to interviewer. The ability to listen and from that to develop different ideas and question different ideas, would enrich my whole career and life.

    In my career, in criminal justice, going to court, meeting people of all levels of education and government, you don't have time to be shy, right?

    I want to be a lawyer. It's so important for lawyers to just be aware of how they're listening to someone. . . . I've interned at places where the lawyers are like writing, mumbling, and the person's telling them a very emotional story of whatever's brought them into the criminal justice system and if you don't even give them that time, that eye contact, just that pause, listen to someone. . . . It's just so valuable, it's going to carry me through the rest of my career.

    [This will] help me communicate clearly to people without expecting them to do the guess-work. I really appreciate this method. It's going to help me a lot in my career.

    These skills will be effective in the legal profession when I'm presenting—by staying away from emotion words, and filling it with more substance, and by layering my stories so they all connect. As I move with purpose I will use that space in a strategic manner.

LIMITATIONS

There are several notable challenges faced when administering this program. First, conclusions about applicability and efficacy should be interpreted with caution as the program was very small and included motivated, established participants. Second, participants were paid for their time with a small honorarium. While individual interview responses indicated that most participants would have participated without monetary remuneration, it is likely that, at least initially, participation was motivated by financial gain. Finally, interview feedback indicated that participants would have liked more explicit connections to content work in classrooms. We concluded that this program could have benefited from being linked to a content course where story prompts could have been explicitly related to course content highlighting themes and encouraging the further exploration of future applicability.

RECOMMENDATIONS

Considering the measured success of this pilot, the author and program developers have identified possible directions for future expansion. We see the main value of the program to revolve around community and cohort building, communications training, and transfer student advocacy. The program applications listed here, which focus on tapping into these outcomes, are not meant to be exhaustive in nature, but instead are meant to inspire explorations for applications relevant to the reader.

- **Transfer Peer Leadership Training**
  At the individual school level, we see a similar storytelling program as applicable to a peer-leader program residing at a community college, four year school, or as a transition between the two. For example, transfer students who have successfully completed the transition to a four-year college could be the target of initial recruitment. The participants could be trained during any Fall semester in storytelling and listening skills and then in the following Spring semester, be employed to apply their skills through mentorship activities like peer advisement. As a final capstone task, program participants could be employed in Summer/Fall Orientation activities for incoming students to present these stories and engage incoming transfers to begin thinking about their own stories. This mentoring application would naturally fit as part of a seminar sequence where storytelling could be related to course content in learning communities or other cohort arrangements.

- **Intern/Extern Led Retention Programs**
  This type of storytelling program could involve a train-the-trainer paradigm for graduate students interested in working with under-

grads in higher education contexts. For example, graduate students in counseling, higher education administration or advising who may be assigned to work with a cohort of vulnerable students may benefit from a listening and storytelling training aimed at engaging struggling students. These skills could be strategically applied to any retention program, "transfer shock" intervention, or skills intervention common for transitioning students.

- **National Advocacy Storytelling Program**

  Focusing more on raising awareness and larger measures of advocacy, any number of schools nationwide could be recruited to participate in a multi-institutional program designed to advocate for general transfer student strengths and successes. For example, a participating college could offer a capstone storytelling program for graduating transfer students who wish to participate or who may have been nominated by a faculty or staff member. Similar to the structure of the current program, five to ten students per school could complete a training sequence with all students from each school participating in a national performance gala as a culminating event. Videos of the stories produced in this national performance could then be available for distribution by way of national educational outlets or organizations such as NISTS.

Cost and Source of Funding

The overall cost of this program was $25,000, which was funded by the Ford Foundation Good Neighbor Committee. It should be noted that a significant portion of the funds were used to rent training space in the heart of Manhattan and this cost could be defrayed if training activities were to be executed on campus. Students were paid around $30 per training session.

REFERENCES

Brown, K. W., & Ryan, R. M. (2003). The benefits of being present: Mindfulness and its role in psychological well-being. *Journal of Personality and Social Psychology*, 84, 822-848. doi:10.1037/0022-3514.84.4.822

Bush, M. (2011). *Mindfulness in higher education*. Contemporary Buddhism, 12(1), 183-197. doi:10.1080/14639947.2011.564838

Fisher, W.R. (1987). *Human Communication as Narration: Toward a philosophy of reason, value, and action*. Columbia: University of South Carolina Press.

Hagen, P.L. (2007, Sept). *Narrative theory and academic advising. Academic Advising Today*, 36(2). Retrieved from: http://www.nacada.ksu.edu/Resources/Academic-Advising-Today/View-Articles/Narrative-Theory-and-Academic-Advising.aspx

Handel, S. J. (2013). *The transfer moment: The pivotal partnership between community colleges and four-year institutions in securing the nation's college completion agenda.* New Directions for Higher Education, 162, 5-15. doi:10.1002/he.20052

Joncich, A. (2013). Mindfulness, role balance, behavioral engagement, and success among college transfer students. (Order No. 3564153, Fordham University). ProQuest Dissertations and Theses, 85. Retrieved from http://search.proquest.com/docview/1402928151?accountid=10932. (1402928151).

Marling, J. L. (2013). *Navigating the new normal: Transfer trends, issues, and recommendations.* New Directions For Higher Education, 162, 77-87.doi:10.1002/he.20059

McDrury, J., & Alterio, M. (2004). *Learning through storytelling in higher education: Using reflection & experience to improve learning.* Sterling, VA: Kogan Page.

Tobolowsky, B. T. & Cox, B. E. (2012). Rationalizing neglect: An institutional response to transfer students. *Journal of Higher Education*, 83, 389-410. doi: 10.1353/jhe.2012.0021.

Walton, G. M. & Cohen, G. L. (2011). *A brief social-belonging intervention improves academic and health outcomes of minority students.* Science, 331, 1447- 1451. doi:10.1126/science.1198364

Adam Joncich *is a program coordinator in the center for academic advisement and new student orientation at Baruch College, City University of New York (CUNY).*

Joshua Henderson *is is a Ph.D. candidate in counseling psychology at Fordham University.*

9

THE INTERSTATE PASSPORT: A NEW FRAMEWORK TO STREAMLINE STUDENT TRANSFER

Patricia Shea and Catherine Walker

STATEMENT OF THE ISSUE

The Interstate Passport Initiative is a grassroots effort that was conceived by chief academic leaders in the WICHE region. This initiative developed a new friction-free framework for block transfer of lower-division general education based on learning outcomes and proficiency criteria at the transfer level. The goals of the initiative are to improve graduation rates, shorten time to degree, and save students' money. Students who earn a Passport at one participating institution and transfer to another will have their learning achievement recognized; they will not be required to repeat courses or other learning opportunities at the receiving institution to meet lower-division general education requirements.

SHORT OVERVIEW

In 2011 members from two WICHE-based organizations, the Western Alliance of Community College Academic Leaders and the Western Academic Leadership Forum (serving two- and four-year institutions, respectively) met with key stakeholders in the West to explore ways to strengthen transfer within and across sectors and state boundaries. Meeting attendants discussed barriers to student transfer and identified opportunities for a voluntary, multi-institution, multistate initiative that would streamline transfer and lead to improved student success and completion. At these academic leaders' request, WICHE manages this multi-state effort as it rolls out the new framework's functionality in phases.

Phase I (October 2011 – April 2014)

Funded by the Carnegie Corporation of New York, Phase I included the development and completion of Passport Learning Outcomes and

Transfer-level Proficiency Criteria in three lower-division areas. Sixteen institutions became Passport signatories, agreeing to award the Passport–and accept Passport transfer students–in Phase I areas. Phase II, funded by the Bill & Melinda Gates Foundation and Lumina Foundation, commenced in October 2014, with institutions in seven WICHE states participating. This two-year phase will conclude in fall 2016 with learning outcomes and proficiency criteria developed for six lower-division general education knowledge and skill areas, completing the Passport framework with a total of nine knowledge and skill areas. The project includes a comprehensive tracking process that collects data on the number of Passports awarded and the academic progress of Passport students, and reports this information to sending institutions and to the Passport Review Board, the project's governing entity.

Program Description

The goal of the Passport is to accelerate and streamline transfer students' pathways to a credential by using learning outcomes and transfer-level proficiency as the currency for transfer. Data from the National Student Clearinghouse show that 33 percent of today's students transfer , with 27 percent of transfers crossing state lines (Hossler et al., 2012). However, only 58 percent of transfers are able to bring all or almost all of credits with them. As high as 28 percent of transfer students lose between 10 percent and 89 percent of their credits (Attewell & Monaghan, 2014). Of particular concern are data from the U.S. Department of Education, which show that more than 81 percent of students who enter two-year institutions intend to complete a degree at a four-year school. However, only 21.1 percent transfer within five years and only 11.6 percent complete a four-year degree (2011). The Passport addresses these obstacles. Students who transfer with a Passport will have their learning in lower-division general education recognized and accepted at Passport-receiving institutions and will not be required to repeat courses. The Passport transfers as a block, so the contents cannot be "unpacked." This interstate block transfer is based on evidence of student proficiency rather than on articulation of specific courses and credit hours.

Knowledge of Concepts and Skills

The Passport encompasses nine lower-division general education knowledge of concept and skill areas, organized as follows:

- **Foundational skills:** oral communication, written communication, quantitative literacy

- **Knowledge of concepts**: natural sciences, human cultures, creative expression, and human society and the individual
- **Cross-cutting skills**: critical thinking and teamwork and value systems.

These academic areas align with the Essential Learning Outcomes of the Liberal Education and America's Promise (LEAP ELOs) developed by the Association of American Colleges and Universities and widely adopted by institutions across the country, (see Figure 9.1 below).

Passport Learning Outcomes and Proficiency Criteria

Passport Learning Outcomes (PLOs) and Transfer-level Proficiency Criteria (PC) were developed in each of the nine Passport knowledge and skill areas. During Phase I the PLOs and PC in the three foundational skill areas were developed by faculty from over twenty two- and four-year institutions from five Western states: California, Hawaii, North Dakota Oregon and Utah. Phase II is currently underway, with faculty participating from those same five states plus South Dakota and Wyoming.

Faculty members from both two- and four-year institutions who teach in each knowledge or skill area, first met within their own states to agree on a "state set" of learning outcomes, derived from institutional learning outcomes for lower-division general education or the state's own general education learning outcomes. Two- and four-year institution faculty representatives from each participating state then convened at the WICHE Learning Center to conduct a "crosswalk" of all states' learning outcomes through which they identify potential learning outcomes that are acceptable across state lines. Faculty members within each content area identified learning outcomes that are in agreement, that that have resolvable differences, and that that have differences that will be difficult to resolve. Through this collaborative process each team produced a draft set of Passport Learning Outcomes, which are vetted with colleagues back home and then finalized. An identical process developed the proficiency criteria.

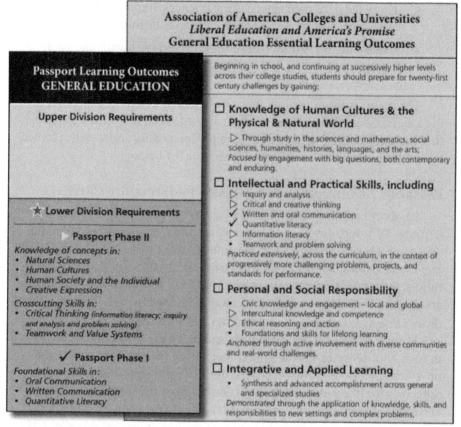

Figure 9.1: Passport Knowledge and Skill Areas and LEAP ELOs

Passport Learning Outcomes are **what** the student knows. The proficiency criteria are **evidence** of proficiency of the learning outcome appropriate at the transfer level that one might see in a student's behavior, performance or work. These are observable behaviors rather than subjective descriptors such as "appropriate" or "excellent." Proficiency criteria are not intended to mandate curriculum or assessment methods, nor do they constitute a comprehensive list that each student must demonstrate. Rather, they serve as examples to faculty of ways for determining whether a student has reached the desired transfer level of proficiency for the specific learning outcome through a variety of possible methods, (see Figure 9.2 below, excerpt from oral communication). Each Passport institution also identifies a list of general education courses and other learning opportunities that impart these learning outcomes at the transfer-level proficiencies, which constitutes the institution's "Passport Block," (see Figure 9.3 below). Through this process, faculty from Passport-participating institutions acknowledge their institutions' lower-division general education learning outcomes in these areas are equivalent to the Passport Learning Outcomes. Institutions are not required to use the same language as the PLOs in their learning outcomes, but ensure alignment to the PLOs.

EXCERPT from ORAL COMMUNICATION		
Passport Learning Outcome Feature	Passport Learning Outcome (WHAT the student has learned)	Transfer-level Proficiency Criteria (EVIDENCE of proficiency of the learning outcome appropriate at the transfer level) *No single student is expected to demonstrate ALL of the proficiency criteria nor is this intended to be a list of all possible proficiency criteria.*
Preparation for Performance	Develop a central message and supporting details by applying ethics, critical thinking and information literacy skills. Organize content for a particular audience, occasion and purpose.	*Student speakers will be able to:* • Select topics that are relevant to and important for a public audience and occasion. • Find, retrieve, and critically examine information from personal experience and published sources for credibility, accuracy, relevance, and usefulness. • Select and critically evaluate appropriate support materials. • Represent sources accurately and ethically. • Become fully informed about the subject matter. • Defend motive of the presentation. • Apply organizational skills in speech writing that use the claim-warrant-data method of argument construction.

Figure 9.2: Excerpt from Oral Communication

Passport Block (Phase I)
Uniquely defined by faculty at each Passport institution

EXAMPLE: North Dakota State University

ORAL COMMUNICATION

- COMM 110 Fundamentals of Public Speaking

WRITTEN COMMUNICATION – Two courses from the following:

- ENGL 110 College Composition I <u>OR</u>
- ENGL 111 Honors Composition I <u>OR</u>
- ENGL 112 ESL College Composition <u>AND</u> ENGL 120 College Comp II <u>OR</u>
- ENGL 121 Honors Composition II <u>OR</u>
- ENGL 122 ESL College Composition II

QUANTITATIVE LITERACY – One course from the following:

- Math 103 College Algebra
- Math 104 Finite Mathematics
- Math 146 Applied Calculus I
- Math 165 Calculus I
- STAT 330 Introductory Statistics

Figure 9.3: Example of Passport Block

The critical role of faculty in the creation of the Passport cannot be overstated. Only faculty have the experience and expertise to determine what learning outcomes should result from general education. Faculty members who impart the knowledge and skills of lower-division general education, who make the assignments, and who assess student proficiency and competency are the best arbiters of the contents of the Passport framework.

A Passport State Facilitator (PSF) in each state serves as the local expert on the initiative, plans all intrastate activities involving stakeholders at participating institutions as well as other interested institutions, and coordinates the involvement of representatives from the partner institutions (and/or others as appropriate) in the interstate activities. As the state's primary representative, the PSF provides the Passport project staff the perspective of constituents in activities leading to eligibility for Passport status. Should institutions in the state be granted Passport status, the PSF serves as his/her state's official representative on the Passport's policymaking body, the Passport Review Board.

TRUST AND TRACKING

The Passport is built on the foundation of trust and tracking. Trust is the understanding that faculty at one institution believe that faculty at other Passport institutions prepare their students to achieve the Passport Learning Outcomes at the proficiency level for transfer. This sense of trust stems from–and is reinforced through–the collaborative process in which faculty engage to produce the PLOs and PC.

Tracking is the process of collecting data to assess the performance of Passport students at their receiving institutions compared to the performance of native students and non-Passport transfer students at those same institutions. The Passport tracking process was developed in Phase I by The Task Force on Student Tracking, comprised of registrars and institutional researchers at Passport institutions. The initial step is to record the Passport in student records. Institutions indicate a student has achieved the Passport by selecting one of three options to record the Passport, as preferred by the institutional registrar:

- **Adding a Comment**: A comment can be added to the transcript to let a transcript processer know about the Passport, when it was achieved and where to find additional information about it.

- **Posting a Pseudo Course**: A pseudo course can be added to the academic history to indicate achievement of the Passport.

- **Creating a Supplementary Record**: An additional record can be created to accompany a transcript sent to Passport Institutions.

Institutions participating in the Passport agree to collect data and provide it annually to the Passport Central Data Repository (CDR) for analysis. Currently Utah State University serves as the CDR for the project.

Passport-receiving institutions collect and share data with the CDR on the academic progress of Passport transfer students and non-Passport transfer students in the first two academic terms after transfer. Receiving institutions provide data in addition to the academic year, term, student category, and other demographic information. Institutions specifically report, for the first two terms after transfer, the number of credits of A, B, C, D, P, Did Not Finish, and F earned at the receiving institution; the mean number of credits earned at the receiving institution; and the weighted number of credits each student completed (mean GPA). The use of course grades at the receiving institution is an accessible proxy for evaluating achievement of proficiency with learning outcomes.

Currently registrars report this information via an Excel spreadsheet tailored to each institution. However, alternative processes are being explored to that might simplify Passport tracking through regular electronic reporting to the National Student Clearinghouse. Understanding the many complications in gathering meaningful data for comparison of Passport students to other students–such as when a student transfers, stopping out, sufficient numbers for comparison–the tracking system will focus on a *representative* sample of similar students at each institution to minimize the impact of uncontrollable variables and maximize the chance that a significant number of Passport students will be included in the data. Passport tracking data may be used by an institution to determine obstacles and inefficiencies, in order to develop appropriate remedies.

The CDR sorts the data from the receiving institutions and forwards it to the relevant sending institutions for use in their continuous improvement efforts. The CDR also forwards aggregate data to the Passport Review Board (PRB) for its annual review of the overall performance of the Passport program. PRB membership consists of the Passport State Facilitators plus higher education experts in academic quality, research, student affairs, and other areas of expertise, and the PBR sets policy and reviews and approves new institutions/states for participation.

During the first year of the project being operational, twelve of the sixteen Phase I signatory institutions submitted data in November to the CDR for Academic Year 2013-2014, establishing a baseline for future data collection and analysis. Passport institutions will collect and report data for the Phase I areas again in November 2015, and in fall 2016 the Passport is expected to be complete. Current and new signatory institutions will award the Passport to students who complete the Passport Block, track Passport students, and collect and report academic progress data on Passport students in all nine Passport knowledge and skill areas.

Benefit to Students, Faculty, and Institutions

Students will know what the lower-division general education requirements are to earn a Passport, and have the guarantee that if they transfer they will not need to repeat learning. Students will not be penalized in the transfer process. For example, if the Passport Block at the sending institution totals nine credits, but the Passport Block/lower-division general education requirements at the receiving institution total 12 credits, the student will not have to take any additional courses to satisfy the requirement. The Passport affirms that the student has fulfilled the requirements at the receiving institution. If the situation were reversed—transferring with 12 Passport/LDGE credits to an institution that requires nine credits in the Passport Block—the extra credits could be applied to an elective or other course. Faculty can make changes in curriculum without triggering articulation review as long as the course still addresses learning outcomes. Institutions also benefit when they receive data on the performance of their former students that can be used to in continuous improvement in advising, transfer policies and procedures.

STRENGTHENING AND EXPANDING THE PASSPORT

Phase II includes plans to invite six states and 12 institutions to join the project from beyond the WICHE region in 2015. Passport staff are working with representatives from the other regional compacts to bring institutions from their member states into the project, including the Southern Regional Education Board, Midwestern Higher Education Compact, and the New England Board of Education.

During Phase II, a robust marketing plan will also be developed and implemented to ensure that students at participating institutions are fully aware of the Passport as they progress through their higher education pathways. Workshops will be held with campus academic advisors and marketing specialists to update them on the Passport and also to solicit their feedback and ideas for keeping students informed. This is an area that needs attention. Recent studies show that students at two-year institutions do not receive adequate guidance about how and if their credits will transfer, and if those credits will count toward a bachelor's degree and program requirements. Too often students make uninformed choices that result in wasted credits and tuition money (Alstadt, Schmidt, & Couturier, 2014).

SUMMARY

Academic leaders throughout the country are developing strategies to increase the proportion of the U.S. population with associate, bachelor's, master's, and doctoral degrees to address the "completion agenda." As a result, states are devoting more attention to the productivity and output of their higher education institutions. Transfer is an essential building block for the completion agenda and integral to the quality and quantity of degree completion. The Passport offers an opportunity to focus on the quality and coherence of learning in lower-division general education across institutions in multiple states. It facilitates transfer across state lines and within states and because it is based on learning outcomes, it adapts to higher education's increased interest in competency-based education. Students achieve the Passport by demonstrating knowledge and/or skills. The Passport is a *block* transfer that cannot be unpacked. Students who earn a Passport at one participating institution and transfer to another will have their learning achievement recognized; they will not be required to repeat courses or other learning at the receiving institution to meet lower-division general education requirements. Implementation of the Passport is expected to save students, institutions, taxpayers and states time and money as it streamlines and accelerates the transfer process, thereby reducing time to credential.

END RESULT AND LESSONS LEARNED

At this writing, the Passport framework is a work in progress, scheduled to be completed and fully implemented in the summer of 2016. Students will require two additional years beyond the implementation timeframe to achieve the learning outcomes, be awarded the Passport, transfer to another Passport institution and complete another two terms of academic work. Until that point, the true effectiveness of the Passport initiative cannot be known. Even so, work on the project thus far has revealed a number of positive outcomes and value to the transfer process.

- Many of the faculty members involved in developing learning outcomes and proficiency criteria, in both Phase I and Phase II, commented on the value of meeting with counterparts from other states for in-depth conversations about learning outcomes and how best to communicate them to students. Interstate conversations between two- and four-year faculty were especially rewarding. This collaborative exercise moved the conversation away from a focus on course titles, numbers, and credits to what kind of learning matters, affirming and rejuvenating those involved, in addition to the value of expertise sharing with lower-division general education faculty who reference the resulting documentation.

- In North Dakota, faculty working on the Passport project are paving the way on state transfer by developing the outcomes and technology that will be needed for the revision of the state's General Education Requirement Transfer Agreement (GERTA). The Passport State Facilitator reports that the Passport tracking system "makes sense" as a model for North Dakota's instate tracking, as it may save actual time and effort down the line.

- Academic advisors at Passport institutions have noted that students value benchmarks on their progress toward degree completion, particularly at two-year institutions. The Passport can serve as a first step toward an associate's degree, providing momentum to students to continue on the path to that degree. In addition, completing general education requirements early in one's academic career allows a student to focus on major courses and requirements.

- The Passport is congruent with a number of national quality initiatives focusing on learning outcomes, including the Liberal

Education and America's Progress, Degree Qualifications Profile, and the Multi-State Collaborative to Advance Learning Outcomes Assessment. All of these projects promote quality and degree completion, and their aligned efforts and products can increase the opportunity for impact of all.

- The currency of transfer has been course equivalencies, determined by faculty and/or registrars at receiving institutions after reviewing course descriptions with their associated seat-time-based credit hours. This process served the system well when institutions had fewer students, fewer transfers, and less record-keeping, and before the significant increase in online learning. Many institutions across the country are now embracing competency-based education in response to demands for more transparency about what students know and can do. The Passport, with its focus on learning outcomes, can serve as a bridge between the credit-based world and the competency-based approaches.

- While states have implemented efficient transfer and articulation policies for instate public institutions, these policies do not address the bigger picture: increased student mobility throughout the country, especially across state lines. Transfer students need to be able to take with them their earned credits, especially in general education, and not be hindered in their pursuit of a degree. The Passport streamlines the cross-state transfer process, acknowledging learning achieved, and keeps transfer students on track.

- The Passport can provide a good foundation for increased focus on pathways. The skills and knowledge contained in lower-division general education is perceived to provide a foundation for success in completing academic work in any major. However, in practice, general education programs are frequently constructed by assembling a menu of courses from across a range of academic disciplines with the expectation that this will provide the student with a solid academic base. The Passport focuses on the learning outcomes that provide this base, and establishes shared learning outcomes through collaborative interactions from faculty across a range of institutions. The Passport is an effective model for the development of degree-specific pathways that are coordinated across institutions.

- Working with faculty and administrators in the development of the Passport framework and processes underscored the need for effective marketing strategies to increase student awareness of the Passport. Students *do* value their accomplishments, but they must know in advance what their options are and how to achieve them. Establishing and maintaining communication with campus academic advisers and marketing specialists will be essential to keeping students informed about the Passport and general education requirements.

- The Passport framework is a faculty-conceived model that addresses an issue, rather than implements a policy imposed by the legislature or other regulatory body. As noted, faculty members involved in development of the Passport highly regarded the opportunity to contribute to and collaborate on a solution for student success.

RECOMMENDATIONS

In addition to working closely with faculty members and others to develop the framework, Passport staff worked with many higher education administrators, associations, and researchers during the four years of the project. A number of recommendations have emerged, including that we need to:

- Don't think about "my students" and "your students" and think about what is best for "our students." The goal of the Passport is to help *students* transfer, to reduce barriers, and keep students on their pathway in higher education, regardless of the institution where they start or end.

- Recognize that "guided" transfer should be an acceptable pathway to graduation and explore more ways to streamline the process. This is particularly needed for students who are STEM majors. To develop a diverse STEM workforce, we must ensure that students who frequently begin at two-year institutions can successfully transfer to a four-year institution and continue on a STEM pathway. There is a need to examine dropout data, especially concerning those students who drop out in their first two years, to determine how transfer might be either a cause or a solution. There is a lack of clarity concerning the reasons around why they drop out, whether it is because they transfer and lose credits (or have to repeat courses) and then cannot afford to continue or what other factors are at play. Students transfer and drop out for a myriad of reasons, and drilling down to identify specific causes and decision points will be useful.

- Work with vendors of student information and degree audit systems to find ways to display student progress toward credentials based on the achievement of learning outcomes. Particularly as competency-based approaches become more widespread, institutions will need to be responsive and prepared to integrate learning outcomes and competencies into student records and SIS programs.

LIMITATIONS

- The Passport is a voluntary program, and institutions must see value in participating. The perceived value will be a factor in the number of institutions that join the project. Some institutions in states where the Passport is underway have not considered signing on to the project because they have few transfer students, or their lower-division general education curriculum needs retuning for learning outcomes.

- Some institutional representatives have not fully grasped the number of degree completers who are transfer students, nor recognized the obstacles that transfer imposes on students. The response of "we don't have a transfer problem" ignores a significant population of students who may have to repeat courses (spending time and money), lose credits, or drop out of college.

- Two-year institutions have a transfer mission, but four-year institutions do not. With the increased emphasis on degree completion, more four-year institutions are now interested in attracting transfer students. But how do institutions support and encourage students to transfer to institutions where they might be better served? A recent study (Velez, 2014) indicated that some low-income and first-generation students would have been more likely to complete their four-year degree if they had begun their studies at a two-year institution. This is an area for future research.

- The Passport tracking and data collection burden can be challenging for registrars at smaller institutions. Plans are underway to address this issue through partnership with the National Student Clearinghouse (NSC). Additional funding is needed, however, to develop NSC Passport-Verify and Academic Progress Tracking for the Passport project.

COST OF THE INITIATIVE AND SOURCE OF FUNDING

- Phase I, October 2011-April 2014, funded by Carnegie Corporation of New York, $550,000.

- Phase II, October 2014-September 2016, funded by the Bill & Melinda Gates Foundation and Lumina Foundation for a total of $2,847,733.

References

Hossler, et al. (2012). *Transfer and mobility: A national view of pre-degree student movement in postsecondary institutions* (Signature Report No. 2), National Student Clearinghouse and Project on Academic Success.

Attewell and Monaghan (2014). The community college route to the bachelor's degree educational evaluation and policy analysis. *American education research journal.*

U.S. Department of Education (2011). Community college student outcomes: 1994–2009, Web Tables. Washington, DC: USDE. Retrieved from http://nces.ed.gov/pubs2012/2012253.pdf.

Alstadt, D., Schmidt, G., & Couturier, L. K. (2014). *Driving the direction of transfer pathways reform: Helping more students achieve their baccalaureate goals by creating structured transfer pathways "With the End in Mind."* Washington, DC: Jobs for the Future.

Velez, E. D. (2014). *America's college drop-out epidemic: Understanding the college drop-out population, national center for analysis of longitudinal data in education research working paper.* Washington, DC: American Institutes for Research.

Institutional Description

Name and Location:
Western Interstate Commission for Higher Education (WICHE), Boulder, Colorado

Institution Type:
Varied, members include fifteen Western states and the Commonwealth of the Northern Mariana Islands

Institutional Selectivity:
Varied

Size of Enrollment:
36,000 students

Patricia A. Shea *is the director of academic leadership initiatives at the Western Interstate Commission for Higher Education.*

Catherine Walker *is the passport project manager at the Western Interstate Commission for Higher Education.*

Section III

Outreach and Advising

The transfer process is inherently complex, and careful planning is essential. Although the diversity of institutions in American higher education is a singular strength, this individuality makes it difficult for students to plan a course of study for more than one institution. To overcome this barrier, the orchestrated cooperation of two-year and four-year institutions in the realm of outreach and advising is a key strategy. Rachel Fulton and Terry O'Brien describe the coordinated efforts of two institutions, Ivy-Tech Community College-Central Indiana (ITCC-CI) and Indiana University-Purdue University Indianapolis (IUPUI), that combined their resources to supply transfer students with the guidance they need to prepare for the pivotal transfer transition. Their work focuses on pre-transfer advising at the community college and also on transitional counseling at the four-year institution, which is needed for students to establish a foundation for academic success.

The importance of counseling at the four-year institution has gained increasing currency among transfer professionals. As noted earlier, four-year institutions set the conditions for admission, obligating them to embrace an active role in providing information to prospective transfer applicants. Kimberly Harvey at the State University of New York at Geneseo and David DeSousa and Luis Rodriguez at Texas A&M each demonstrate the pivotal importance of advising at the four-year institution. Harvey focuses on the development of the "You Belong" Program, which provides an opportunity for new transfer students to connect with other transfer students and access a network of individuals who can help them adjust to the four-year college. DeSousa and Rodriguez describe a series of advising and recruitment efforts focused on the specific needs of transfers, including program-planning material, course equivalency information, and guaranteed admission.

An often-mentioned problem with the transfer process is the degree to which students "lose credit," at the receiving institution after transfer. Without fully aligned articulation agreements between two- and four-year institutions, transfer students are at the mercy of *ad hoc* judgments about the acceptability of their coursework from the community college. Loss of credit—whether it occurs as non-acceptance of coursework outright by the four-year institution or a failure of the institution to apply community college work for anything other than elective credit—slows student progress and may discourage them from completing the four-year degree. Brianna Larson of Utah Valley University tackles this issue, describing a series of steps her institution has initiated to create articulation agreements in majors conferring a Bachelor of Fine Arts. Through consultation with faculty at neighboring community colleges and faculty leaders at her institution, Utah Valley University was able to create clear course pathways for students in areas that have been traditionally difficult to align between two- and four-year institutions.

Westchester Community College's Robin Graff and Jennifer Blalock from Phi Theta Kappa address the importance of embedding transfer best practices in every aspect of the community college. Graff and Blalock delve into the possibilities for creating more intentional opportunities for early and effective transfer engagement, in order to avoid the "transfer traps" of taking excess credits, leaving prerequisites unmet, or creating unnecessary financial burdens. The chapter explores the importance of teaching, advising, communicating, promoting, and incentivizing transfer in order to best assist students through their entire academic journey.

The focus shifts to the roles and responsibilities of private institutions as a transfer destination with Beth Zielinski from the Jack Kent Cooke Foundation and Nancy Sanchez from the Kaplan Educational Foundation. Their work focuses on how to best support low-income, high-potential, historically underrepresented community college students at private institutions. Although nationally community college transfer students tend not to attend private institutions, Zielinski and Sanchez suggest that potential under-matching of high-achieving community college students can be avoided with high-touch, proactive, and consistent advising that continues beyond the point of transfer into the four-year institution and through to graduation. This longitudinal approach across institutional boundaries best assists transfer students as they learn to navigate the complex new environment of an elite, private institution.

10

Establishing Effective Transfer Partnerships

Rachel Fulton and Terry O'Brien

Abstract

As the landscape of higher education continues to evolve with a focus on completion and performance-based funding, Indiana University–Purdue University Indianapolis (IUPUI) recognizes the value of the transfer student and intentionally focuses on this population. As a result of strategic planning in early 2013, the IUPUI Office of Transfer Student Services and the IUPUI & Ivy Tech Coordinated Programs (Passport) Office co-located on the IUPUI campus to facilitate a seamless pathway and handoff from Ivy Tech Community College–Central Indiana (Ivy Tech–Central Indiana) to IUPUI. With over half of external transfer students coming from Ivy Tech–Central Indiana, this advising and programming collaboration is integral to fostering a successful transition.

Pre-transfer and transitional advising are pertinent for transfer students as they negotiate the environment of a new institution (Flaga, 2006; Handel, 2007). This article provides an overview of the programs and services that each office offers, with a focus on advising on both campuses. Also explored are the day-to-day functionality of the shared office space and the strategic joint partnerships for student success. These partnerships are illustrated with specific examples offered by the Office of Transfer Student Services and promoted by the Passport Office, such as Transfer Tuesday. Readers are presented a replicable framework for potential implementation at their institutions.

Statement of the Issue

Transfer students comprise over one-third of the Indiana University–Purdue University Indianapolis (IUPUI) undergraduate student body (with nearly 60% of our transfer students from Ivy Tech–Central Indiana), thus supporting students both pre- and post-transition is pivotal to their success. Navigating new academic, social, and physical environments that differ significantly from the community college creates barriers for transfer students (Flaga, 2006). Two offices are dedicated to serving transfer students and assisting in the transition: the Office of Transfer Student Services and the IUPUI & Ivy Tech Coordinated Programs (Passport) Office. Together, these offices support students by offering opportunities related to advising, involvement, and unique IUPUI expectations.

PROGRAM DESCRIPTION

Changes in the higher education landscape–especially concerning an increased focus on college completion rates and student mobility–have placed student transfer between two- and four-year institutions in the spotlight. Examining promising transfer practices is essential as greater numbers of colleges and universities work with this underserved population. On the Indiana University–Purdue University Indianapolis (IUPUI) campus, the offices dedicated to this student population are the IUPUI & Ivy Tech Coordinated Programs Office (Passport Office) and the Office of Transfer Student Services.

Transfer-serving Offices at IUPUI

The IUPUI & Ivy Tech Coordinated Programs (Passport) Office was created in 1990 as a unit in the Division of Enrollment Management at IUPUI with a dual reporting line to Academic Affairs at Ivy Tech–Central Indiana. The office: (a) "ensure[s] general coordination between [the two institutions] with regard to credit courses, non-credit courses, student services, needs assessment, and marketing..."; (b) "monitor[s] and help[s] promote coordinated student services to facilitate student transfers, concurrent enrollment, and course credit transfer"; and (c) "promote[s] both institutions as distinct post-secondary institutions with differentiated missions which collaborate to meet the full range of community needs" (IUPUI & Ivy Tech Coordinated Programs, 2015; Davies, 1999; Townsend & Wilson, 2006). A director, an assistant director, and an academic advisor staff the Passport Office. Additional student staff includes a program coordinator for diversity initiatives, a project specialist, an information specialist, and a receptionist.

The Passport Office supports prospective transfer students in a variety of ways, focusing on pre-transfer advising and transfer-specific programming. Pre-transfer advising occurs both on the Ivy Tech–Central Indiana and IUPUI campuses. The academic advisor spends 80% of his or her time on the Ivy Tech–Central Indiana campuses advising (via appointment and walk-in sessions) current students who intend to transfer to IUPUI. The assistant director is also cross-trained in pre-transfer advising and meets with Ivy Tech students on the IUPUI campus by appointment. As a part of pre-transfer advising, advisors:

- Discuss the student's intended major at IUPUI,
- Evaluate current Ivy Tech courses,
- Discuss how Ivy Tech courses distribute into the IUPUI major (including applicable articulation agreements),
- Plan future courses to be taken at Ivy Tech prior to transfer, and
- Share involvement opportunities on the IUPUI campus for prospective transfers.

The Passport Office is responsible for additional advising-related components including outreach to students who were deferred admission to IUPUI, managing the Guest Student Application process for those IUPUI students planning to take a course on the Ivy Tech campus concurrent with their enrollment at IUPUI, and developing articulation agreements in collaboration with faculty from both campuses.

The Passport Office provides Ivy Tech–Central Indiana students intending to transfer to IUPUI with a variety of programming designed to foster early integration in the community. Ivy Tech–Central Indiana hosts transfer fairs every semester to provide current students an opportunity to speak with representatives from a variety of four-year institutions. The Passport advisor along with a member of the IUPUI Office of Undergraduate Admissions team and other academic unit advisors/recruiters represent IUPUI at these events. Additionally, the assistant director coordinates targeted campus visits for specific Ivy Tech–Central Indiana student groups. These visits are tailored to the unique needs of the student group and include a personalized, transfer-focused campus tour, a lunch in the premier student dining facility with current IUPUI students, and presentations related to their specific transitional experience (such as the Office of Student Financial Services and The Multicultural Center). In an effort to foster early integration into the IUPUI community, the Passport Office connects similar student groups on each campus, introducing the leadership of each organization and helping to coordinate a common event hosted by the Passport Office. These programming activities combine with pre-transfer advising to provide a foundation for seamless transition to IUPUI.

The Office of Transfer Student Services was created in early 2012 under the IUPUI Division of Undergraduate Education and was charged to: (a) "serve as a central hub for transition programming and service provision..."; and (b) "provide campus-wide coordination and leadership for serving the large population of transfer students that make up the student body of IUPUI" (Transfer Services Strategic, 2012, p.3). In its current form, the office "support[s] all transfer students, after the point of admission, by facilitating seamless pathways and encouraging programming and resources to ensure successful transition, persistence, and graduation" (Transfer Student Services, 2015). The office partners with campus departments and schools to promote services and programming designed to facilitate the academic and social integration of transfer students to the IUPUI campus (Davies, 1999; Flaga, 2006; Townsend & Wilson, 2006). Two full-time professional staff the Office of Transfer Student Services: a director and a transfer coordinator. Student mentors are awarded scholarships in exchange for their assistance with programming.

The Transfer-Year Experience (TYE) is a key focus of the Office of Transfer Student Services, and is designed to respond to the unique needs of transfer students. The TYE provides support, programming and involvement opportunities designed to enhance how transfer students connect to IUPUI. The TYE includes, but is not limited to:

- "Finish at IUPUI" Facebook group – an opt-in group dedicated to serving transfer students (prospective, entering, and continuing), returning adult, and veteran IUPUI students;

- Transfer Tuesday – transitional advising webinars designed to enhance the academic advising experience prior to orientation;

- Transfer Student Orientation – a program coordinated through the Office of Orientation Services including an Academic Prep Session immediately before the students' one-on-one advising appointments;

- T-Shirt Swaps – held each fall and spring semester, entering transfer students have the opportunity to bring a t-shirt from their previous institution and swap it out for a brand new, free IUPUI t-shirt;

- Transfer Insider – an electronic newsletter sent throughout the semester that informs students about campus events and campus resources, and provides valuable tips on being successful at IUPUI;

- Transfer Seminar – a transitional course in the major taught by an instructional team consisting of a faculty member, academic advisor, librarian, and an experienced student mentor; and

- Other school-based initiatives (e.g. Pathways to IUPUI: Social Work) – when requested by the academic school, the Office of Transfer Student Services collaborates to facilitate school-determined outcomes through a unique experience.

Ultimately, these support programs and resources enhance students' academic integration, social integration, and self-efficacy on the IUPUI campus.

Strategic Partnerships

In early 2013, the IUPUI Office of Transfer Student Services and the Passport Office were combined into one space on the IUPUI campus to facilitate a seamless pathway from Ivy Tech–Central Indiana to IUPUI. Utilizing Flaga's (2006) work on the transition of community college students, the offices strive to remedy issues students face through the five dimensions of transition (learning resources, connecting, familiarity, negotiating, integrating) within all three environments (academic, social, physical). The offices primarily assist in navigating the academic environment via academic advising. The Passport advisor provides tools (learning resources) for both Ivy Tech–Central Indiana and IUPUI and develops working relationships (connecting) with prospective students. This familiarity prepares students for the handoff that will come at the point of admission, and decreases the time spent navigating and integrating within the academic environment on the IUPUI campus. The Office of Transfer Student Services also facilitates transition during Transfer Tuesdays. Both offices assist students in understanding the physical environment of the IUPUI campus, both pre- and post-transfer. Through targeted campus visits, the Passport Office introduces students to the physical spaces (learning resources) they will be navigating and help them make connections to important spaces where their majors are housed or where services exist. The Transfer Student Orientation at IUPUI is focused on the connecting dimension, and the T-Shirt Swap or Transfer Seminar is designed with the familiarity dimension in mind (McGill & Lazarowicz, 2012; Schlossberg, 1984), with a primary focus on the social environment. All programs facilitate transfer student peer contact to help "meet people and develop relationships with fellow students" (Flaga, 2006, p. 8). Campus visits with the Passport Office are done in groups and feature interaction with current IUPUI students. The "Finish at IUPUI" Facebook group allows students to connect with each other on social media. Transfer Seminars have a capped enrollment of 25 students and utilize a peer mentor in the major, creating a more intimate environment.

With a significant portion of transfer students originating from Ivy Tech–Central Indiana, advising and collaborative programming are integral to the success of these students. The joint suite for the two transfer-serving offices is located on the first-floor of a classroom building adjoined to a first-year student residence hall. The Passport portion of the suite consists of the director's office, a cubicle for the assistant director, and a shared cubicle space for the academic advisor and information special-ist, a reception desk, and a large collaborative workspace in the center. The Office of Transfer Student Services has an office inside of this suite shared by the director and transfer coordinator. The receptionist is funded through the Passport Office, and is cross-trained to welcome all visitors regardless of the office they are seeking. Information sharing is vital to the success of the shared space and strategic partnership. For example, cross-promotion of programs creates a more seamless transition for Ivy Tech–Central Indiana transfer students. Programs such as Finish Fridays (transfer campus visits), Pathways to IUPUI: Social Work (TYE experienc-es for human services students transferring into the social work program), and Transfer Tuesdays (transitional advising webinars) are successful because of the open information sharing and cross-communication. The professional staff regularly meets to discuss independent office programs and services, to develop a personal rapport and to help ensure a positive working environment. These personal relationships combine with knowl-edge sharing to foster the strategic partnership across divisions.

A program that exemplifies the strategic partnership between the Of-fice of Transfer Student Services and the Passport Office is Transfer Tues-day, a weekly post-admission transition-planning webinar. Transfer Tues-day helps admitted students understand how their credits have transferred to IUPUI and prepares them for their orientation advising appointment (Ott & Cooper, 2013). While at an Ivy Tech–Central Indiana pre-transfer advising appointment, the Passport advisor lets the student know they are expected to participate in one of these webinars upon admission to IUPUI. This expectation is viewed as another mandatory step such as attending orientation or submitting final transcripts. Once a student is admitted to IUPUI, the student receives an electronic communication from the Office of Transfer Student Services that discusses the webinar and the potential benefits of Transfer Tuesday. The webinars take place via Adobe Connect and features a synchronous presenter, a slide deck for con-tent delivery, and a chat space for student-student and student-presenter interaction. Sessions occur every Tuesday at various times.

The content of the Transfer Tuesday webinars include the transfer credit report, the undistributed credit process, degree plans, and next steps to be completed prior to the orientation advising appointment. Completing a Transfer Tuesday helps students evaluate how their credits transferred, explain undistributed versus distributed credit, describe the process for resolving undistributed credit, and outline the advising re-sources available to help them succeed. The program is assessed through a mixed-methods survey focusing on achievement of the learning outcomes and general satisfaction with the session. This survey duplicates questions from the Transfer Student Orientation Exit Survey to help assess improvement across similar learning outcomes.

IMPACT AND END RESULT

The strategic partnerships between the Office of Transfer Student Services and the Passport Office have a constructive impact on students and their transition and success at IUPUI. As Allen, Smith, and Meuhleck (2014) note:

> Like a relay race where both runners are responsible for the baton and hold onto it during the handoff to insure that it is not dropped in the transition, student success in the transition from community colleges to 4-year institutions results from collaborative efforts between the two types of institutions (p. 364).

Open communication allows for each office to understand the programs and services of their counterpart and simultaneously builds a comprehensive resource base for students. Collaborative programming is then the metaphorical handoff mentioned in the quote above.

The Transfer Tuesday preliminary program survey results show that students who participated in this program were satisfied with the advising they received. In the first seven sessions, there were 74 registrants. Of the 35 participants, 26 responded to the program survey distributed immediately following the session. Respondents strongly agreed or agreed that they are able to evaluate how their credits transferred (96%) and explain the process for resolving undistributed credit (96%); they were able to explain the difference between distributed and undistributed credit (92%); and they were able to outline the advising resources available to help them be successful (88%). The questions mirroring the Transfer Student Orientation Exit Survey received positive results as well with respondents strongly agreeing or agreeing: they were active participants in the session (88%); working with an advisor will be an important part of their college experience at IUPUI (100%); as a result of the session they are familiar with the requirements for their degree program (77%); and the session improved their understanding about how their transfer credits articulated to IUPUI (96%). Though only 47% of the registrants have attended to date, it is important to note that a high number of those who registered but did not attend reregistered for a future session. Aggregate Transfer Tuesday data will be compared to Transfer Student Orientation Exit Survey data at the end of the pilot, slated for the end of orientation season. Ultimately, individual students participating in a Transfer Tuesday will be tracked for retention, persistence, and graduation and compared to those students who did not participate as well as those who registered but did not attend.

RECOMMENDATIONS AND LIMITATIONS

To develop strategic partnerships among transfer-serving offices on a four-year campus or between the community colleges and the four-year institutions, sharing physical space is key to effective collaborations. Co-located space is beneficial as it naturally creates conversations and opportunities for information sharing. Importantly, transfer students looking for support during their transition only have one stop to make. If a shared space is not feasible, finding collaborative space should be prioritized. Another alternative might be to rotate locations between the two office spaces, whether on the same four-year campus or on two separate campuses.

Beyond space, interoffice and interpersonal components should be addressed. Regular meetings should be held in order to foster good rapport across offices. These meetings should focus on three elements: sharing individual programs/services, investigating collaborative opportunities, and getting to know each other as people – "identify[ing] their strengths, passions, and skills" (Bloom, Hutson, & He, 2008, p. 43). Developing this rapport will assure the other elements will be easier to accomplish. Whether in person or electronic, information sharing and transition planning will naturally be facilitated. The student will benefit from the underlying relationships with consistent access to institutional knowledge (Flaga, 2006). The strategic partnerships would not be possible without institutional assistance. Support from administration at both institutions–or in this case, both divisions–creates a positive and collaborative environment. If an office similar to the Passport Office does not exist at your institution, develop similar buy-in with the administration at the sending/receiving institution to facilitate the partnership. Similarly, if a transfer center does not exist on the four-year campus, it is crucial to develop relationships with the academic schools or transfer admissions representatives.

Institutions looking to implement a transitional advising program similar to Transfer Tuesday should be aware of several key issues. The technological, human, and time resources required to create the experience need to be considered. Does the institution have appropriate technologies (e.g. Adobe Connect) to host webinars? Who will be responsible for facilitating the sessions each week? What times and days work best for the students at your institution to participate? Should there be pre-transfer institution-specific sessions (e.g. specific sessions for Ivy Tech–Central

Indiana vs. open sessions for all transfers)? What advising resources are pertinent to be shared prior to a first advising experience versus what content can wait until orientation? How will you evaluate the effectiveness of the program for your students?

Although IUPUI has increased its efforts to support transfer students, this work has limitations. One limitation is the lack of a direct student handoff between the Passport advisor and the student's academic advisor at IUPUI. Until the student is admitted to IUPUI, the Passport advisor is unable to determine whether or not the student is directly admitted into their major school or to University College. In addition, many majors have multiple advisors and each academic school organizes advising caseloads differently. Although the Office of Transfer Student Services attempts to assure the transition is as seamless as possible, the advisor-to-advisor transition needs to be improved. A second potential limitation within the strategic partnership is the necessary rapport between offices. The partnership only functions as well as the relationship: director to director and transfer coordinator to assistant director and academic advisor. Special attention must be invested in these relationships, as they will ultimately dictate how openly information is shared and the level of investment in cross-promotion and co-programming. A third limitation is the limited number of staff dedicated to serving transfer students compared to the size of the population served. A small staff can be a limitation when designing new programs and services to foster transfer student success. However, the current shared physical space would not be able to support an increase in the staffing structure.

FUNDING SOURCES

The Division of Undergraduate Education is funded through the Indiana University Responsibility-Centered Management (RCM) model. Through this budget model, the Office of Transfer Student Services receives its operational funding allocation from the General Fee and academic school generated funds. The IUPUI & Ivy Tech Coordinated Programs (Passport) Office falls within the Division of Enrollment Management at IUPUI with a dual reporting line to Academic Affairs at Ivy Tech–Central Indiana. The Division of Enrollment Management is also funded through the Indiana University RCM model. Through this budget structure, the Passport Office receives 50% of its budget from the IUPUI base budget. Ivy Tech–Central Indiana then matches IUPUI Division of Enrollment Management's budget contribution at 100%. All programmatic costs for each office come solely from these two office discretionary budgets, and no additional funds are provided for programming.

References

Allen, J. M., Smith, C. L., & Muehleck, J. K. (2014). Pre- and post-transfer academic advising: What students say are the similarities and differences. *Journal of College Student Development, 55*(4), 353-367.

Bloom, J. L., Hutson, B. L., & He, Y. (2008). *The Appreciative Advising Revolution*. Champaign, IL: Stipes Publishing, L.L.C.

Davies, T. G. (1999). Transfer student experiences: Comparing their academic and social lives at the community college and university. *College Student Journal, 33*(1), 60.

Flaga, C. T. (2006). The process of transition for community college transfer students. *Community College Journal of Research and Practice, 30,* 3-19. Doi: 10.1080/10668920500248845

Handel, S. J. (2007). Second chance, not second class. *Change, 39*(5), 38-45.

IUPUI & Ivy Tech Coordinated Programs (2015). Your connection to IUPUI & Ivy Tech. Retrieved from http://passport.iupui.edu/

McGill, C. M. & Lazarowicz, T. (2012). Advising transfer students: Implications of Schlossberg's transition theory. In T. J. Grites, and C. Duncan (eds.) *Advising Student Transfers: Strategies for Today's Realities and Tomorrow's Challenges* [Monograph No. 24]. Manhattan, KS: National Academic Advising Association.

Ott, A. P. & Cooper, B. S. (March 2013). They're transfer students, not cash cows. *The Chronicle of Higher Education*. Retrieved from http://chronicle.com/article/They're-Transfer-Students-Not/137935

Schlossberg, N. K. (1984). *Counseling adults in transition*. New York, NY: Springer.

Townsend, B. T. & Wilson, K. B. (2006). "A hand hold for a little bit": Factors facilitating the success of community college transfer students to a large research university. *Journal of College Student Development, 47*(4), 439-456.

Transfer Services Strategic Planning Group (2012). *Enhancing support for transfer students at IUPUI*. Unpublished, University College, Indiana University Purdue University Indianapolis, Indianapolis, Indiana.

Transfer Student Services (2015). About us. Retrieved from http://transfer.iupui.edu/AboutUs/PurposeObjectives.aspx

INSTITUTIONAL DESCRIPTION

Name and Location:
Indiana University–Purdue University Indianapolis (IUPUI), Indianapolis, IN; Ivy Tech Community College–Central Indiana (ITCC–CI), Indianapolis, IN

Institution Type:
Public, urban, Research I four-year, high graduate coexistence (Master's/Doctoral); Public, urban-serving single campus, two-year, exclusively undergraduate

Institutional Selectivity:
selective; open admissions

Size of Enrollment:
Over 30,000 students, Enrolling more than 30,000 students

Rachel Fulton *is the transfer coordinator in the office of transfer student services at Indiana University-Purdue University Indianapolis (IUPUI).*

Terry O'Brien *is the assistant director of the IUPUI & Ivy Tech coordinated programs office at t Indiana University-Purdue University Indianapolis (IUPUI).*

11

LOOKING THROUGH THEIR LENS: AN ASSESSMENT PROJECT OF SPRING TRANSFER STUDENTS

Kimberly A. Harvey

STATEMENT OF THE ISSUE

Approximately 60% of university graduates nationwide complete degrees with credits from more than one institution (Adelman, 2006). Furbeck (2011) found the following factors important to transfer students during the transfer process: affordability, number of credits accepted at receiving institution, quality of the academic major, and the timeliness and accuracy of information received. Assessing the experiences of transfer students as they face academic, social, and personal challenges in their transition to a new institution provides data crucial to improving transfer student retention, persistence, and well-being.

SHORT OVERVIEW

SUNY at Geneseo's *YouBelong* program provides an opportunity for new transfer students to connect with each other and access a network of faculty and staff knowledgeable about SUNY Geneseo. *YouBelong* seeks to ease the transition of transfer students into the Geneseo community.

This program runs throughout the academic year in order to accommodate both Fall and Spring transfer students. The *YouBelong* program comprises academic and social programming throughout the transfer student's first semester at SUNY Geneseo.

The *YouBelong* program series:

- acknowledges the needs of transfer students by providing programs that address academic, social, and transitional issues,
- informs students of campus facilities, college offices and services, and other essential information through regular communication with transfer students,

- presents opportunities for transfer students to socialize and interact with other Geneseo students and develop academic and co-curricular interests through informational sessions and workshops, and

- provides individual guidance and support to all transfer students during the transition process.

PROGRAM DESCRIPTION

During Spring 2008, the Department of Residence Life had a unique opportunity to work with and study 220 Spring residential transfer students as they moved into a newly-reopened residence hall. Residence Life staff members gathered information from this cohort of residential transfer students in order to conduct research with the goal of improving retention and graduation of future transfer students at the college. During the Fall 2008 semester, two pilot programs were designed for new transfer students. The first program, a "Transfer Student Mixer," was designed to address the social transition of new transfer students. A second program, "Pre-Advisement and Course Registration," focused on the process and importance of meeting with an academic advisor to select courses for the following semester.

In response to the evaluations of these two pilots programs and to address the social and academic transitional needs of transfer students to Geneseo, *YouBelong*: Connecting Our Undergraduate New Transfer Students or COUNT was created in January 2009. *YouBelong* was created in response to the evaluations of the two pilots programs mentioned above. The core mission of *YouBelong* is to welcome new transfer students and help them feel a sense of belonging to their new college.

The *YouBelong* series is scheduled and details are confirmed for each program prior to the start of the semester. Primarily a collaborative effort between Residence Life and New Student Programs, *YouBelong* also involves additional campus departments, including the Office of the Dean of the College (Academic Affairs), Career Development, Campus Auxiliary Services, Geneseo Opportunities for Leadership Development (GOLD), and Student Life, that also contribute to *YouBelong*. Some programs included in the *YouBelong* series already exist on campus (e.g., student organization fair, volunteer fair, and leadership workshops), whereas others have been specifically designed for transfer students. All programming supports the goals of *YouBelong* and assists in meeting the needs of our transfer students' academic success and social integration.

While transfer student are not required to reside on campus, many transfer students decide to live on-campus when they first transfer to Geneseo. During the Fall 2009 semester, the Department of Residence Life made a decision to house transfer students in "blocks," thus creating mini-cohorts of transfer students living together. This cohort model has proven successful, as it helps to forge connections among transfer students and fosters a strong sense of belonging in the campus community. Moreover, we have seen an increase in leadership positions held by transfer students (e.g., hall council positions, Resident Advisors). The *YouBelong* programs are staffed by Undergraduate Resident Advisors (RAs) and Orientation Advisors (OAs), who have successfully completed the transfer process. The RAs and OAs serve as a team of transfer student connectors (i.e., near-peer mentors) who recommend *YouBelong* programs and workshops, as well as host and promote the programs. These student staff members work to coordinate the series each semester with the Director of New Student Programs and a Residence Director, who oversees residence halls that include a transfer student "block." The programming primarily focuses on the first six weeks of each semester when transfer students are most eager to connect with other transfer students and are most likely to ask for help.

Each semester, promotional materials are designed, printed, and distributed to all new transfer students. The materials feature the scheduled workshops and events, and include important college contacts and dates.

In the Spring 2013 term, the Department of Residence Life and the Office of New Student Programs conducted an assessment of residential students admitted to the college. This assessment project was a follow-up to the study conducted in Spring 2008 when our residence hall reopened after renovations. The planned January 2013 reopening of Monroe Hall (where newly-admitted transfer students were going to be housed) provided an opportunity to learn about the transfer student experience, especially those who entered Geneseo through the Guaranteed Admissions Program (GAP).

Resident Assistants were trained to conduct interviews, and throughout the month of March 2013, the RAs interviewed Spring admits with a standard instrument. In total, 242 out of 332 spring transfer students participated in an interview, a 73% participation rate. Names were not included on the survey answers, but students were given the option of identification if they wished to enter a drawing for a gift-certificate for participating in the survey.

We hoped this assessment would provide insight into how our campus was meeting our cross-departmental Student and Campus Life outcomes:

- SUNY Geneseo students will successfully complete the transition to college life.
- SUNY Geneseo students will develop leadership skills, and apply them in both the collegiate setting and their communities upon graduation from Geneseo.

It was hoped standardized, face-to-face interviews conducted by resident assistants to Geneseo GAP students and other transfer students admitted to the College in the Spring 2013 term would provide insight into the experience of being a mid-year admit, inform our campus-specific knowledge of the social and academic transition needs of transfer students, provide data to refine our leadership development programs, and assist in gauging the level of healthy behaviors during a transfer student's first semester at Geneseo.

END RESULT AND IMPACT, LESSONS LEARNED

When students were asked why they chose to attend SUNY Geneseo, four themes emerged: reputation, quality of education, affordability, and campus/community atmosphere. The majority of students indicated the quality of the education and the programs offered combined with the reputation of the college were their main reasons for attending Geneseo. Students noted that Geneseo was an affordable option, especially considering the perceived quality of the academic programs. The final theme centered on the beauty of the campus and the community atmosphere. A strong sense of campus community made students feel welcomed and influenced their decision to attend Geneseo.

This assessment indicated Geneseo's *YouBelong* program successfully increased mid-year transfer students' sense of academic and social connection on campus. Participation in GOLD, a leadership program open to all students, jumped from 11% in 2008 to 20% and this is likely attributable to the highlighting of leadership opportunities in *YouBelong* programming. A positive increase of surveyed students expressing satisfaction with advising and scheduling improved from 54% (2008) to 64% (2013). This was attributed to the Dean of Curriculum & Academic Services' work with transfer students and the *YouBelong* co-sponsorship of programs with the Office of the Dean.

Both the 2008 and 2013 studies confirmed many mid-year transfer students flourished because they were able to live together in a newly reopened residence hall. Although these were rare opportunities due to renovation, Residence Life should operationalize the positive nature of the shared residence hall experience by creating spaces where Spring transfer students connect with each other. This is currently achieved in the standard "transfer floors" reserved for Fall admits; but the department should continue its efforts for Spring admits. One possibility is to carve out space via a mid-year housing consolidation, although this is not popular with students who are asked to move when they lose a roommate mid-year. Additionally, Residence Life should assure online information for mid-year admitted transfer students is available and accurate by October each Fall, as approximately a third of students reported using the Residence Life and housing websites.

During the 2013 interview, Spring admits were asked if they identified as a "Geneseo student" or a "transfer student." We wanted to know at what point in their transition students stop referring to themselves as a "transfer student" and began to use the general term, "Geneseo student," so we asked participants to comment on what factors relate to this distinction. 128 students referred to themselves as a Geneseo student, ninety students referred to themselves as a transfer student, and twenty-four students did not respond. Students who entered Spring 2013 have had a positive experience with their transition to Geneseo. They identified and participated in opportunities to get to know their professors, make friends, learn about navigating campus, living with a roommate, and feeling connected to the campus community. The trends discussed below also emerged when asking students about their transition to Geneseo.

Transfer of Courses, Advisement, and Registration

The responses varied when students were asked about their advisement and registration experiences. Some students shared that they were satisfied with the information provided to them and the registration process. Although most rated their advisement experiences positively, the comments described the advisement and registration processes as confusing, rushed, and stressful. Some students felt they were placed into wrong classes and believed class options were limited due to late registration. Some students found their advisers to be supportive, helpful, and honest, but negative comments included dissatisfaction with advisers and the overall January registration experience. Many students stated that they were misinformed or pushed into decisions, that their advisers seemed to lack enthusiasm and that the advisors did not seem to care about their input.

Academic Transition

The responses among students were split in regards to academic transition to Geneseo. Many found classes to be more rigorous but they are able to manage their workload. While classes are challenging at Geneseo, many students responded that the expectations are achievable and that they are figuring out how to be successful. In contrast, other students found their classes to be too demanding, overwhelming, and requiring too much work. These students found the academic transition difficult and were adjusting to the rigor of Geneseo coursework. Some struggle because of the ambiguous expectations and because deadlines and exams sometimes tended to occur in the same week.

Relationships with Professors

The responses provided by students about the relationships they have built with faculty ranged from positive to negative. Students mentioned having personable professors who are open-minded, approachable, available, and helpful. Some commented that relationships with professors are better in smaller class-size settings. In contrast, some students had yet to establish relationships with their professors, especially in large lecture-style classes and stated that their professors seemed to be standoffish, less friendly than at other institutions, and unclear about expectations.

Social Fit, Making Friends

Students provided an array of comments on making friends at Geneseo and finding their social niche. Students from Monroe Hall found that living in the building among other new mid-year transfer students helped them easily make friends. Students explained that the Geneseo community is warm and welcoming, that they feel they are a part of the community, and that they had no trouble making friends. Some students mentioned that they wished they had lived in Monroe, while others mentioned that they want to branch out beyond the Monroe community. Many students included comments about awkward relationships with roommates, discomfort with being known as a transfer, feeling self-conscious about transitioning halfway through the year, and having a desire to "branch out more fully." Some students were in the process of "finding their fit" and developing Geneseo school pride.

Campus Involvement and Navigation

When asked about navigating the Geneseo campus, some students responded that they find navigating the campus easy. They believe the campus is intimate and find people were willing to help if someone was confused or lost. Other students mentioned that they still get lost on campus, or had trouble in the beginning of the semester but have a better grasp on navigating the semester after asking for help or referring to maps.

Overall, we saw a need to address the transfer student experience at SUNY Geneseo. Studying the cohort of mid-year admits in Spring 2008 and Spring 2013, provides the necessary feedback to continue refine our intentional program to address the identified social, academic, and transitional needs of our transfer student population. Each semester we have adjusted the *YouBelong* series based on student feedback and program evaluation.

RECOMMENDATIONS AND LIMITATIONS

This assessment focused on traditional-aged mid-year admits who lived on campus in residence halls. The 149 students who were interviewed lived in a residence hall together as a mid-year cohort, and the findings may be limited to these contexts. Despite these limitations, this assessment provides insight into the needs of mid-year admits.

Currently, there isn't a transfer center at Geneseo, but the majority of respondents indicated they would visit such a center to seek academic and social resources. Of our sample of Spring admits, 62% would be "likely" to "very likely" to utilize a Transfer Student Center (TSC). While the majority of Spring admits would utilize such a dedicated space, some students expressed a concern that a TSC would isolate transfer students even more from the overall Geneseo community.

An overarching theme in our Spring admit survey was of students not feeling informed, combined with a lack of communication about events, resources, and deadlines. Students enumerated resources they would hope to find in a Transfer Services Center. Responders wanted a "one-stop shop" with an adviser, a place to go for assistance with advisement, registration, transfer credit information, and major requirements. Similarly, students wanted a transfer counselor—someone to help with transfer-related questions, and miscellaneous information, such as navigating the institutional web resources, developing housing plans, or simply offering advice. A help desk was also recommended, staffed with transfer or upper class students who could serve as mentors or tutors to incoming transfer students. Aside from advisement and transfer counseling, students believed a Transfer Services Center could serve as an information hub for job opportunities, campus maps, information about clubs/organizations, and general campus resources. An ideal environment would include a study area, computers and should serve as a welcoming space for students to connect and make friends.

Mid-year admits were very confident in their academic abilities, with an 86% confidence rate for keeping up with course requirements. However, similar findings among new transfer students suggest a "first-semester naïveté," often referred to as "transfer shock" (Glass & Harrington, 2002). Subsequent study is needed to measure the GPAs of mid-year admits to determine how their self-appraisal and confidence levels actually compare to academic performance.

The assessment was used to rationalize the creation of a transfer resource space that officially opened in October 2014. This dedicated space, combined with the expansion of the program series, has led to an increase in transfer student engagement and attendance.

COST OF THE INITIATIVE AND SOURCE OF FUNDING

The cost to run the *YouBelong* programming series for an academic year is $5.50 per student, based on 500 transfer students. The program utilizes workshops/programs and staff members already available on-campus. This approach provides a cost-effective means for providing programming especially for new transfer students. A new student picnic (Fall semester) and dinner (Spring semester) is a highlight of the series, and is subsidized by students through the use of their own meal plans, while the remaining costs of the program are shared by the Office of New Student Programs and Department of Residence Life.

REFERENCES

Adelman, C. (2006). *The toolbox revisited: Paths to degree completion from high school through college.* Washington, DC: U.S. Department of Education.

Furbeck, L. F. (2011). Enrollment management of transfer students. In M. A. Poisel & S. Joseph (Eds.), *Transfer students in higher education: Building foundations for policies, programs, and services that foster student success* (Monograph No. 54, pp. 13-28). Columbia, SC: University of South Carolina, National Resources Center for The First-Year Experience and Students in Transition.

Glass, J. C., & Harrington, A. R. (2002). Academic performance of community college transfer students and "native" students at a large state university. *Community College Journal of Research and Practice, 26*(5), 415-430.

INSTITUTIONAL DESCRIPTION

Name and Location:
The State University of New York (SUNY) at Geneseo, NY

Institution Type:
four-year, residential, public liberal arts college

Institutional Selectivity:
highly selective

Size of Enrollment:
5,500 students

Kimberly A. Harvey *is the director of new student programs at the State University of New York at Geneseo*

12

Steering Transfer Student Towards the Right Path: Advising and Recruitment Strategies Used at Texas A&M University

David De Sousa, Jr. and Luis Rodriguez

Statement of the Issue

The Office of Admissions at Texas A&M University is striving to increase the number of qualified transfer students who enroll at the university, while continuing to improve their recruitment, advising, and counseling efforts and practices. Initiatives have been put in place to attract high achieving transfer students while providing them with a transfer-friendly admissions process.

Short Overview

In order to enhance Texas A&M University's (TAMU) advising and recruitment efforts, the Office of Admissions has provided students with three tools that help them navigate the process. The university has provided these prospective students with transfer course sheets, a transfer course equivalency website, and an articulation agreement called the Program for Transfer Admission (PTA), which provides a guarantee of admission into certain majors. In addition to these tools, denied freshman applicants have the option to pursue an alternative admission option which also carries a guarantee of admission.

Program Description

For the past several years the university and its administration has been actively engaged in seeking out and implementing the best strategies to help with the mission of being known as a transfer-friendly institution. The Office of Admissions has implemented several strategies to aid in this process. These strategies include the transfer course sheets, a transfer course equivalency web page, and the Office of Admissions articulations agreements.

Students interested in seeking transfer admission to Texas A&M University are encouraged to plan early and connect with one of the counselors who are able to guide them through the process. To be considered for transfer admission to Texas A&M University, students must have at least a 2.5 grade point average (GPA) on a minimum of 24 hours of graded, transferable coursework. Selecting a major is the first component in the transfer process because each major has its own transfer admission requirements. For this reason, the Office of Admissions has worked closely with the academic colleges to create the transfer course sheets which provide the student with all of this crucial information. These sheets provide future transfer applicants guidance on coursework selection as well as GPA suggestions. It is to a student's advantage to follow the guidelines and complete courses as outlined on the transfer course sheets in order to be the most competitive applicant.

In addition to the transfer course sheets, the Office of Admissions partnered with the academic colleges and created a transfer course equivalency website located on the transfer admissions webpage. This tool contains a searchable database of course equivalencies/evaluations from colleges and universities across the nation. Students can either select "search by sending institution" or "search by Texas A&M course number." The evaluation of courses on the transfer equivalency website is a guide, and transferability of any given course is not guaranteed until evaluated upon application; however, it is a helpful resource that can give the students an idea of how courses have transferred in the past from those particular institutions. Specific course equivalencies require review based upon the unique characteristics of each college and university and may differ from one institution to another.

In addition to these campus-based strategies, Texas lawmakers have also implemented statewide initiatives designed to strengthen transfer. Senate Bill 175—commonly referred to as the "Top Ten Percent Transfer Rule"—was recently enacted and provides a guarantee of transfer admission for eligible high school graduates. Transfer applicants who graduated from a Texas high school and were ranked in the top ten percent of their class may qualify for automatic transfer admission to Texas A&M University if they complete the core-curriculum at a public **junior** college or other public or private **lower-division** institutions in Texas with a 2.5 GPA on a four-point scale or equivalent.

To address these issues, Texas A&M has created some unique partnerships not only locally with Blinn College (Blinn TEAM), but also with every community college district in the state of Texas (Program for Transfer Admission). The Blinn TEAM, which is a collaborative effort between the local community college (Blinn College) and Texas A&M University, has been in existence for over fifteen years and was the first of its kind in the country. It is an outstanding example of collaboration between institutions and has since become a model for other universities to follow. The collaborative efforts of eight of the universities in the Texas A&M University System and Texas A&M University have also led to the creation of what is known as the Program for System Admission. There is also a number of scholarship opportunities created specifically for prospective transfer students. In addition, the university has created several transition and retention initiatives to increase transfer student success.

Program for Transfer Admission

The Program for Transfer Admission (PTA) offers prospective transfer students a unique opportunity to be automatically admitted to Texas A&M University. PTA is designed for students attending Texas community colleges and offers more than sixty-five degree plans. Upon successful completion of the coursework outlined by the major coursework check sheet and additional requirements of the program, participants are eligible for automatic admission to Texas A&M.

Below are the requirements and guidelines for this program:

- Complete all required paperwork for the program and attend a mandatory academic meeting with a Texas A&M University admissions counselor.
- Choose and complete all program-specific coursework requirements, from one of the PTA degree plans for the proposed major choice.
- Complete at least thirty transferable hours after high school graduation at any Texas community college within three years from the date on which participation begins.
- Maintain a minimum 3.2 cumulative GPA.
- Earn a grade of a "B" or better in all bold, italicized coursework specified in the degree plan.
- Submit all other required documents (application fee, transcripts, essay, etc.) by the appropriate deadline for admission to Texas A&M University.
- Participants will be "grandfathered" into PTA under the degree plan which was in place at the time of signature on the participation form.
- Participants may only sign up for PTA once.
- The most recent consecutive 30 transferable hours must be done in residence at any Texas community college or combination of Texas community colleges.

- Participants may mix and match coursework from different Texas community colleges.

- Bold, italicized graded coursework in the degree plan may only be attempted once (excluding grades of W and WP).

- If a participant earns a grade of a "C" or lower in the bold italicized coursework (including dual credit), the participant will not be admitted via PTA but is still eligible for traditional transfer admission.

- Participants are allowed a maximum of three withdrawals (W's) throughout their college career.

- There are no coursework substitutions.

- Participants applying for fall admission may submit final spring grades by June 1, for consideration.

- AP Credit cannot be used to satisfy a required course (bold, italicized) for PTA.

Program for System Admission

In addition to the PTA, the Office of Admissions also created a program called the Program for System Admission (PSA). This program is for students that were not fully admitted as an incoming freshman. Through this alternative admission program, selected students may enroll in one of the Texas A&M University System Institutions that participate in PSA with the goal of returning to Texas A&M University in College Station after successful completion of their first year in college.

Below are the guidelines for this program:

- Students must have a complete freshman application for the fall semester on file with the Office of Admissions at Texas A&M University in College Station by December 1st.

- Students must meet the minimum requirements for admission to the Texas A&M System Institution they wish to attend.

- Students must respond to the PSA offer via the Applicant Information System (AIS) by May 1st.

To qualify for automatic admission via the PSA, students must meet the following criteria:

- Choose and complete specific course requirements from one of the approved TAMU program-specific degree plans.

- Complete at least 24 transferable hours in residence at a system institution during the fall and spring semesters.

- Maintain a minimum 3.0 cumulative GPA at the System Institution and maintain a minimum 3.0 cumulative GPA on all transferable coursework (including dual credit taken during high school).

- Submit all required credentials by the published deadline.

It is recommended that developmental course(s) and/or prerequisite course(s) be taken prior to fall enrollment. For example, some institutions require College Algebra or other developmental courses before enrolling in higher level math courses. The goal of developmental courses is to help students work up to college level courses. In most cases, students taking developmental courses have more individual faculty attention. They help provide students with the opportunity to have a successful college career.

The Blinn Team

Another option offered to incoming freshmen applicants is Texas A&M Blinn Team. The Texas A&M Blinn TEAM ("Transfer Enrollment at A&M") Program is a collaborative, co-enrollment partnership between a major university (Texas A&M) and a community college (Blinn College). Each year since 2001, this pioneering initiative has allowed the admission of hundreds of additional qualified students into the Texas A&M freshman class that would have otherwise not been possible due to enrollment limitations.

Participating students are initially admitted to Texas A&M University on a part-time basis, and may earn full admission by several methods. TEAM students are enrolled in one academic course at Texas A&M each semester, and complete the remainder of their courses at the Bryan Campus of Blinn College. Students who complete 45 Blinn credit hours and 15 A&M credit hours within a two-year period, while maintaining a 3.0 GPA at each school, are automatically admitted to Texas A&M. TEAM students who wish to transition to A&M sooner may compete for transfer admission if they meet the university minimum transfer requirements. Finally, students who do not transition by the aforementioned methods may become eligible for future admission as returning former students via the university's readmission process (subject to current readmission criteria).

TEAM students benefit from enrollment at both institutions; students enjoy the university experience afforded by Texas A&M (such as residence hall life, sports events, and a huge range of student activities), while enjoying the smaller classroom environments and costs of Blinn College. Academic advisors, faculty, and staff at both schools facilitate TEAM student successes. TEAM was the first program in Texas to connect a junior and senior institution in exactly this way.

The Texas Higher Education Coordinating Board complimented the TEAM Program in 2013 by bestowing "Recognition of Excellence." In 2014 TEAM received the Board's coveted "Star Award" as one of the top educational initiatives in Texas.

Transfer Scholarships

Additionally, Texas A&M also offers transfer scholarships specifically for high achieving Phi Theta Kappa members. The TAMU Phi Theta Kappa Transfer Scholarships are designed to recognize outstanding transfer students who will be attending Texas A&M University. Students must transfer directly from a Texas community college and have been actively involved with the Phi Theta Kappa chapter associated with their campus immediately prior to transfer. Students must complete at least twenty-four hours at their previous community college and maintain a minimum 3.0 GPA while at Texas A&M University. The awards range in value from $1,500 to $10,000 dollars annually and are renewable for up to two years. Selection criteria for the Phi Theta Kappa (PTK) Transfer Scholarship include, but are not limited to, academic achievement, extracurricular activities, leadership, PTK involvement, academic major, and, in some instances, financial need as determined by the Free Application for Federal Student Aid (FAFSA).

Eligibility:
- The student must be a Texas resident.
- The student must be a first time undergraduate degree seeking transfer from a Texas community college.
- The student must be an active member of the Phi Theta Kappa chapter associated with the community college from which they are immediately transferring from.
- To renew, each semester recipients are required to maintain enrollment in at least 12 credit hours in both the fall and spring semesters, a minimum cumulative GPA of 3.0, and not be on conduct probation. This scholarship is renewable for up to two years, or four semesters.

By offering this scholarship, Texas A&M University has seen an increase in the number of Phi Theta Kappa students applying to the university. Based on internal records, in the 2013-2014 school year, the university received a total of 875 Phi Theta Kappa applicants, by the 2014-2015 school year this number had increase to 998.

Post-Transfer Strategies

On top of these strategies, Texas A&M University offers an array of programs that are designed to help reduce the effects of "transfer shock" that incoming students may experience. These programs include T-Camp, Howdy Camp and the New Transfer Student Conference. Transfer shock refers to the tendency of students transferring from one institution of higher education to another to experience a temporary dip in GPA during the first or second semester at the new institution (Hills, 1965). Culture shock is a condition of disorientation affecting someone who is suddenly exposed to an unfamiliar culture, way of life, or set of attitudes. These issues cannot be ignored, and consequently, Texas A&M has created several programs to address these pervasive problems.

Transfer Camp (T-Camp) is an organization designed to foster a meaningful experience for incoming transfer students. Members are responsible for creating an inclusive atmosphere that introduces campers to the many opportunities and traditions that exist at Texas A&M University. Through this process, campers enhance their Aggie network by creating relationships that strengthen and define the true essence of the Aggie Spirit. The students get the opportunity to meet other incoming transfer students, as well as those current students who previously came to the university as transfers.

Howdy Camp is a student-run orientation program for new Aggies planning to attend Texas A&M University in the spring semester. This camp includes transfer students as well as freshmen students and is the spring semester's equivalent to T-Camp. It is held over a three-day period in January immediately before the spring semester begins. During this time, new Aggies are introduced to the many traditions, indescribable spirit, and customs of Aggieland. Speakers and special interest programs are brought in to inform students of the endless activities and opportunities available to them at A&M and in the Bryan-College Station community.

To officially accept an offer of admission, all students must register and attend a New Student Conference (NSC). During the NSC, students receive orientation materials and official conference schedule. Students have the opportunity to participate in campus tours, engage in resource tables where they will learn about different services for students on campus, and meet with their academic advisors to help register for courses. Family members and guest are also encouraged to attend the NSC with their newly admitted Aggie.

Texas A&M recently established The Academic Success Center, which is a collaboration between Academic Affairs and Student Affairs. Using a holistic approach, the Academic Success Center helps students identify roadblocks to academic success and ensures that all students have access to comprehensive resources. With the success of the Academic Success Center, Texas A&M wanted to provide a unit on campus designed to enhance the transfer student academic experiences at the university. The Transfer Student Program (TSP) is a program designed for incoming transfer students to learn more about the resources at TAMU and make connections with other transfer students, faculty, and staff, as well as actively encourages engagement at all levels of the university.

Transfer students sometimes face unique challenges that may only become apparent as the semester progresses; the TSP eases the transition into Texas A&M University. The university offers social and academic support throughout the semester to students in all colleges and majors. On staff, there are a number of Transfer Student Peer Mentors (TSPM) from a variety of colleges. Formerly transfer students, they are extensively trained and hold office hours. They will do their best to help provide students answers to questions, resources, and encouragement so that the students may get the most out of their experience at Texas A&M University.

Transfer students are quickly becoming a center of attention at many universities today. The above models are transferable and are an innovative set of programs that other universities could replicate for transfer student success. Taking advantage of social and academic enhancement programs at the university level can be one of the most memorable parts of a college experience.

End Result and Impact, Lessons Learned

According to the American Association of Community Colleges (2014), two-year institutions are especially attractive to a wide diversity of students given their open access admissions policy. In Texas, the popularity of community colleges is on the increase, given lower tuition costs compared to four-year institutions and the opportunity for students to prepare for transfer to a four-year college or university. For these reasons, Texas A&M University is working to strengthen its partnerships with Texas community colleges. The success of this effort is reflected in the steady enrollment increase of transfer students to Texas A&M (see Table 12.1). The transfer student enrollment numbers suggest that the pre-advising and recruitment strategies at Texas A&M are working. The university is continually looking for innovative solutions to increase the quality and quantity of its student body.

Table 12.1
3 Year Enrollment Transfer Report

Year	Enrolled
2012-13	2945
2013-14	3282
2014-15 (Summer not included)	3297

Source: http://dars.tamu.edu

RECOMMENDATIONS AND LIMITATIONS

In order for these initiatives to be more effective the authors recommend the following concepts:

- Introduce these programs at an early stage to community college students and faculty/staff.
- Go beyond the community college arena and engage high school students about these programs.
- Encourage students to meet with admissions advisors at the university at an early stage.
- Visit the university, these programs are working, but in order to increase enrollment the authors believe that visiting the campus would increase distinguishability.
- Spread the message that articulation agreements are formal "guaranteed" agreements. Every student and parent likes to hear the word "guaranteed."
- Encourage current and prospective transfer students to become transfer ambassadors for these programs.
- Actively communicate with academic departments across the university regarding transfer student recruitment and retention resources.

After analyzing these programs, the authors did not know how popular these programs would become. The enrollment for these programs were higher than estimated. The demand is still high while transfer student enrolment continues to grow. Other units on campus had to be involved in order to operate these programs smoothly. It is recommended that partner institutions become very transparent when working in collaboration with each other.

FUNDING

Texas A&M University has three sources of available funding: state funds, the Available University Fund (AUF), and local funds. Each funding source is subject to specific rules regarding how it may be used. A portion of the returns from the Permanent University Fund (PUF) are annually directed toward the AUF. The University of Texas System and The Texas A&M University System split the AUF on a two-thirds and one-third sharing ratio, respectively (Texas A&M Essentials, 2011).

The Permanent University Fund is a public endowment contributing to the support of institutions of The University of Texas System and institutions of The Texas A&M University System. The PUF was established in the Texas Constitution of 1876. The local funds are collected locally by the university (Texas A&M Foundation, 2015).

REFERENCES

AACC. (2014). Fast facts from our fact sheet. Retrieved from http://www.aacc.nche.edu/AboutCC/Pages/fastfactsfactsheet.aspx

Hills, J. R. (1965). Transfer shock: The academic performance of the junior college transfer. *The Journal of Experimental Education, 33* (2), 201-215.

Texas A&M Essentials. (2011). Financial resources. Retrieved from

http://provost.tamu.edu/essentials/pdfs/FinancialResources-Factsheet_072011.pdf

Texas A&M Foundation. (2015). Frequent Asked Questions. Retrieved from http://www.txamfoundation.com/s/1436/gid3give/2014/index.aspx?sid=1436&gid=3&pgid=2285

INSTITUTIONAL DESCRIPTION

Name and Location:
Texas A&M University (Land, Space and Sea Grant)

Institution Type:
Public, four-year

Institutional Selectivity:
Competitive admissions

Size of Enrollment:
47,567 (Fall 2014)

David De Sousa, Jr. *is a senior regional advisor at Texas A&M University.*

Luis Rodriguez *is a senior admissions counseling advisor at Texas A&M University.*

12

EFFECTIVE TRANSFER ARTICULATION SEQUENCING FOR IMPROVED GRADUATION RATES

Brianna J. Larson and Dane Abegg

STATEMENT OF ISSUE

Students transferring to Utah Valley University from Utah community colleges lose credit due to the lack of intentional articulation and misaligned course sequencing. Numerous courses receive elective credit or remain unapplied to the student's degree. Due to differences in course offerings and availability, students are unable to use all of their transfer credits towards their UVU degree.

OVERVIEW

Comparing and evaluating programs offered at the community college with current UVU degree pathways, advisors and department chairs were able to effectively award equivalent transfer credit towards the UVU program. Course sequencing sheets were created that designated the specific community college transfer courses students needed to complete in order to be awarded full transfer credit and to seamlessly transfer into upper division courses at the university level.

PROGRAM DESCRIPTION

The School of the Arts at Utah Valley University serves 33,000 students, including 2,000 dedicated majors. In a review of issues within the California system, Hagedorn (2006) states, "As more and more students elect to attend the country's network of two-year institutions, the importance of assisting students to succeed on the path that leads through the community college to bachelor degree attainment is more pronounced" (p.224). As an institution committed to student success and engagement, Utah Valley University's Academic Advisors noticed a trend of unapplied or general nonspecific elective credit being awarded to students transferring from Utah community colleges. An examination of the evaluation process was undertaken to see if credits could be more effectively awarded and to learn if the misalignment between the university and community college system might be rectified with the creation of course sequencing sheets for this specific student population.

Holding to the mission of the university to provide opportunity and promote student success, the Dean agreed with the need to strengthen pipelines of enrollment from the community college as well as to increase diversity, promote engagement, further inclusiveness, and foster completion, due to the documented "lower rates of bachelor's degree completion among students starting their educational journeys in community colleges. . . students who begin their educational journeys in 2-year institutions seem to have a lower likelihood of bachelor's degree completion" (Roska, 2011). Recognizing the possible marginalization of transfer students, the School of the Arts was determined to correct perceived issues in the transfer articulation process.

In an effort to make the community college to university transfer experience a seamless one, academic advisors, department chairs, and the dean determined that changes to the transfer articulation agreement would provide the most effective means of helping students, especially if students were unable to access assistance with the transfer process at the community college. The literature on the transfer student experience has discussed reasons for transfer issues, reasons including effective dissemination of transfer requirements for the community college student. As stated by Hagedorn (2006), "For most community college students, counseling is key to obtaining the knowledge that will lead them through the community colleges. Unfortunately, counseling is a rare commodity" (p. 239). While the relationships among the School of the Arts advisors and community college counselors have been strong, there seemed to be high levels of need for student academic advisement in the community college system. Furthermore, community college students in the arts may not receive the discipline-specific support they need, or they might not know how to ask for the proper support with transfer planning.

University academic advisors noticed the trend of discriminate transfer articulation while working with students throughout their academic careers. Succinctly stated by Laanan, Starobin, and Eggleston (2010), "working with students individually, counselors will be better informed about transfer students' issues and concerns and will be better prepared to assist students in their social, psychological, and academic adjustment process." (p. 196). Advisors were tasked to be the initial point of contact for department-specific student services; they noted a repetitive pattern for students negatively affected in the transfer process. Students transferring from the community college to the university were analyzed by admissions in both qualitative (academic advisement appointments, curriculum content, and portfolio reviews) and quantitative (transcript data, articulation agreements) ways. Upon analysis, transfer discrepancies were most notable with illustration majors in the Bachelor of Fine Arts program; for example, the community college program required three separate courses focusing on the Adobe Creative Suite: Photoshop, Illustrator, and InDesign, whereas the University teaches the Creative Suite in one course. Although these students had gained content area learning, they were not receiving credit when they transferred. Community college students began to successfully challenge the university course.

Based on curriculum review of the community college courses and established mastery of concepts as reflected by transfer student portfolios, the department chair and advisors approved a change to the articulation agreement that allowed the trio of community college courses to fulfill the single university course. Another instanced involved the figure drawing courses. The figure drawing course at the community college was not transferring to the university, despite a similar curriculum and course structure. Wanting to ensure that students weren't repeating lower division courses, and recognizing the need for community college students to quickly move into a more technical, comprehensive, and industry-related bachelors program in the arts, the UVU visual arts department decided to accept the community college courses in figure drawing and advanced figure drawing as fulfilling the required figure and anatomy drawing course. This curriculum adjustment concurrently satisfied an important prerequisite for upper division figure courses and completed a requirement for the Bachelors of Fine Arts program or an elective for the general art degree.

It is vital to understand the cost-analysis model developed by Lang (2009) to understand why transfer articulation needed to be maintained. Community colleges are typically touted as a less expensive entry into post-secondary education; however, barriers in transfer articulation routinely prove the opposite. Lang (2009) notes that although community college may seem to be a less expensive route, "we know that students who transfer, even in highly articulated systems, do not transfer all credits, and take some remedial courses that do not generate credit at all… Thus, to the student, transfer is almost always more expensive than direct entry to university even if it seems less expensive to the government. This is sometimes called the 'diversion affect' of transfer. It is real, and students and counselors understand it" (p. 368).

This divergent affect was highly apparent to the university advisors working with transfer students. Students transferring into the university's illustration program from the community college art program were losing their Adobe suite and figure drawing credits. This loss totaled five classes, or a semester worth of tuition. This also did not take into account any individualized remedial courses or additional electives the student might have completed that were also unapplied. By working to improve transfer articulation, the university was able to bring projected tuition costs for transfer students down to nearly identical rates for those who started at the university.

Furthermore, a transfer-specific course sequence sheet was developed for distribution to art major community college students. Community college advisors would be able to disseminate accurate information about correct course offerings and ordering to students in order to foster the most seamless and effective transfer process possible.

The Theatrical Arts and Music programs also discovered a set of community college courses that were not being awarded equivalent university credit. Those courses were reevaluated, and the departments developed additional course sequence sheets for the community college programs that focused on the most efficient application of the open-ended elective options for the associate's degree. The new course sequence sheets identified the best course options for community college that would simultaneously apply to their degree while also satisfying specific requirements for the university programs in theater and music.

End Result and Impact, Lessons Learned

The re-evaluation of transfer credit courses, articulation agreements, and the creation of course sequence sheets provided students a smoother transfer experience and a clearer pathway to graduation by maximizing their time and money spent at both the community college and the university. Assessing student needs and course outcomes uncovered more optimal equivalencies between the two- and four-year institutions. Academic advisors were keenly aware of the financial costs to their arts-seeking majors and wanted to assist with supporting the talents and passions of the students. Due to the sensitivity of faculty, chairs, dean, and other administrators, this articulation restructuring provided streamlined pathways to success and strengthened transfer for a unique and diverse body of community college students.

After this update, the university was able to apply 95% of the transferred community college major coursework to equivalent courses. Administration and faculty gained a deeper appreciation for community college programs, as their curriculum was demonstrated to clearly align and articulate with university courses. Students clearly benefited, as completed lower division prerequisites now clearly transfer with a seamless matriculation into upper division courses.

Cost of Initiative and Source of Funding

No additional cost (other than regular salary of faculty, administration, and support staff) was required. The department and university share a dedication to engaged learning, and staff are expected to work on individual projects that positively influence student satisfaction, retention, and graduation rates.

References

Hagedorn, L. (2006). Transfer between community colleges and 4-year colleges: The all-american game. *Community College Journal of Research and Practice, 30*(3), 223.

Laanan, F. S., Starobin, S. S., & Eggleston, L. E. (2010). Adjustment of community college students at a four-year university: Role and relevance of transfer student capital for student retention. *Journal of College Student Retention: Research, Theory & Practice, 12*(2), 175-209. doi:10.2190/CS.12.2.d

Lang, D. W. (2009). Articulation, transfer, and student choice in a binary post-secondary system. *Higher Education, 57*(3), 355-371. doi:http://dx.doi.org/10.1007/s10734-008-9151-3

Roksa, J. (2011). Differentiation and work: Inequality in degree attainment in U.S. higher education. *Higher Education, 61*(3), 293-308. doi:http://dx.doi.org/10.1007/s10734-010-9378-7

Institutional Description

Name and Location:
Utah Valley University, Utah

Institution Type:
Public, Master's Comprehensive

Institutional Selectivity:
Open Admissions

Size of Enrollment:
31,332 undergraduate enrollment

Brianna J. Larson *is an academic advisor at Utah Valley University.*

Dane Abegg *is an academic advisor at Utah Valley University.*

13

COMMUNITY COLLEGE TRANSFER PREPARATION: INTENTIONAL OPPORTUNITIES FOR EARLY AND EFFECTIVE TRANSFER ENGAGEMENT

Jennifer L. Blalock and Robin Graff

ORGANIZATIONAL DESCRIPTION

Phi Theta Kappa is one of the nation's oldest and largest honor societies, and is credited as the official honor society recognizing community colleges by the American Association of Community Colleges. Its mission is two-fold:

1. To recognize and encourage the academic achievement of two-year college students, and

2. To provide opportunities for individual growth and development through participation in honors, leadership, service and fellow-ship programming. An international organization, its headquarters are located in Jackson, Mississippi. There are currently over three million Phi Theta Kappa members, worldwide, with chapters at two-year degree granting institutions in all fifty states and in eight countries.

PROGRAM OVERVIEW

The onset of spring frequently fosters a campus-wide sentiment of excitement, with impending completion and graduation for many community college students. It also tends to foster anxiety over next steps and concern about whether there has been adequate preparation for the university transfer process. Community college transfer personnel, advisors, counselors, and faculty are often inundated by students–including high achieving ones–frantically attempting to address the gaps in the transfer experience which they haven't anticipated. From higher tuition costs to unmet prerequisites, the community college transfer student can easily find herself overwhelmed by the complicated process of transitioning from a two-year institution to a four-year institution. To empower community college transfer-bound students with the resources necessary to successfully navigate the transfer process, early interventions and collaborative planning are encouraged. There are best practices available that can be adapted and implemented by two-year institutions.

PROGRAM DESCRIPTION

Appreciating the complexity of transfer preparation for community college students requires that two-year institutions provide early and frequent interventions, exposure to and engagement with proven best practices. Establishing standards of behavior for the community college transfer-bound student at the outset is key.

Introduce and Integrate Transfer from Day One

Wherever appropriate, introduce and integrate transfer elements into widely-used student services. Transfer preparation components may enhance such campus programming as community college orientation, student success workshops, and welcome back programs. Whenever possible, consider integrating dedicated transfer offices or areas into the One-Stop Student Services office placement. Moreover, including transfer pathway information as part of the community college admissions process is another key touch point for beginning the transfer process early and effectively.

Talk & Train Transfer

Academic and faculty advisors hold substantial responsibility for connecting students to their transfer options. Because of this, they must be well-prepared and trained about the institution's existing transfer relationships. This requires intentional transfer training; opportunities to attend national, state, and local transfer-focused conferences; and relationship-building networking opportunities with college and university transfer colleagues and peers. Community college advisors should be encouraged to regularly and consistently emphasize community college completion and transfer options as motivational aspects of the advisor/advisee relationship.

First Advisement

First Advisement frequently encompasses program advisement, degree requirement review, and course selection, while also providing an opportunity to begin introduction of elements critical to transfer success. Based on institutional procedures, first advisement may take place as a component of orientation, in small group advisement cohorts, or in individual advisement sessions. Regardless of the format, the following components are recommended as essentials of first advisement:

- Connection of community college degree progress with college/university program admission requirements
- Identification, review, and discussion of student short-term (community college) and long-term (university transfer) goals, as well as intended professional objectives
- Introduction of a wide-ranging discussion including:
  - Articulation agreements and university transfer pathways
  - Which selected community college courses fulfill both community college degree completion and transfer prerequisites
  - Next steps and action items for students to explore and research as they build their personal knowledge base of university transfer relationships and awareness
- Transfer Fairs
- College Visits
- Second and subsequent advisement sessions
- Online research
- Statewide transfer websites and resources

Teach Transfer

Preparing faculty of cornerstone and foundational coursework about the transfer process and training them about established transfer pathways encourages the faculty to foster a strong sense of classroom connectivity that reinforces the importance of proactive behaviors. Ideal classes for transfer curricular integration include first-year experience, career exploration, leadership, orientation, composition, and student success classes. Collaborating with academic leadership to incorporate transfer training in faculty workshops, trainings, and professional development activities as a regular component creates and sustains awareness and builds a shared responsibility in educating students in this area.

The Transfer Academy Model

Several two-year institutions in Texas, including Austin Community College and Tarrant County College, have introduced Transfer Academies. These free multi-session events are composed of three to five intentional workshops that are scheduled during a "dead hour" on campus. Topics highlight campus resources, such as the Writing Lab for assistance in writing scholarship or transfer essays and personal statements, and also include off-campus resources, inclusive of university scholarship offices and study abroad programming. Students who complete all transfer academy sessions offered each term may receive a certificate and are entered into a drawing for a $500 scholarship.

Campus-wide Collaboration and Beyond

Having established how important advisors and faculty are to promoting best transfer practices, it is important to include other departments on campus that may also offer substantive contributions to transfer preparation. Several offices and departments also have transfer outcomes and objectives, including as Athletics and TRIO. By combining efforts and sharing resources, collaborative transfer workshops and events can be even more successful and effectively implemented. There are also off-campus opportunities that may enhance the transfer programming, including pre-professional groups, economic development offices, and career and workforce programs.

Pee-to-Peer Transfer Touches

Community college students are predominantly first-generation college students, and many never envisioned themselves completing a two-year degree. Contemplating a four-year degree requires the navigation of more academic, personal, and psychological barriers. Seeing peers successfully graduate and transfer to a four-year institution can be extremely motivating and inspiring to other students from class or the tutoring center. Showcasing such successes on social media, in college publications, and at transfer events creates a sense of possible reality for students who may have considered transfer a distant dream. If possible, create and connect students early on so they have a network of familiar faces and peer recommendations to ease their transfer transition.

The True Cost of Transfer

Achieving admission to a coveted four-year college academic program is only part of the journey. Many community college students find their joy at admission cut short when they realize they haven't adequately prepared for the increase in costs, tuition, and fees related to transfer. Beginning these discussions early on in advisement, workshops, and curricular content helps expose students to scholarship eligibility and often encourages them to get more active on campus – both inside and outside of the classroom.

Take Transfer on the Road

Transportation to university or college campuses can sometimes be a challenge for community college students with limited options and funds. First-generation students may especially be overwhelmed by the size, scope, and procedures of the larger university or college to which they are hoping to attend. Consider approaching student organizations and/or requesting activity funds to subsidize small group trips to nearby colleges and universities.

Leverage Transfer Technology

While nothing beats a physical tour of a campus, there are limitations of both time and cost that prohibit students from visiting all of their potential transfer institutions. Several free online transfer-focused resources exist to help promote and empower community college transfer-bound students. CollegeFish.org, powered by Phi Theta Kappa, is a free online resource that connects community college students to over 2000 regionally accredited four-year colleges and universities, as well as over $37 million in transfer scholarships. This database is also free and available to community college transfer personnel to aid them in guiding students throughout the transfer process, and includes a course planner, transfer calendar, college comparison chart, and milestone management tools to keep students on track toward achieving completion and transfer goals.

Communicate and Promote Transfer

There's no shortage of important information being communicated to community college students through a myriad of media. From text messages to college-wide emails to the old-fashioned letter, students are bombarded with information and are often confused about where, when, and how to use it. Consider creating an institutional timeline of key points throughout the academic calendar for effective touches, to craft meaningful "calls to action" that promote completion and transfer preparation, and to identify the most effective ways to connect with the students.

Incentivize Participation

Whenever possible, connect students to potential outcomes and additional opportunities by participating in the various transfer planning and preparation activities. Students respond positively to incentives and outcomes that reveal a positive result or return from their investment, so the institution might showcase a student leader who has been awarded a generous transfer scholarship to a prestigious college or university, or procured an award or prize from a campus partner.

Westchester Community College: Best Practices in Action

Creating a list of transfer interactions is just one part of the process. Building these processes into the daily practice of transfer programming requires a dedicated, committed team of stakeholders. At Westchester Community College, Transfer Services serves a diverse, dynamic student population at one of SUNY's largest two-year institutions. The staff, including a director and an assistant coordinator, appreciates the importance of creating a transfer culture that is seamlessly integrated into the fabric of the institution. The Transfer Services Office offers an ambitious, multi-faceted year-long calendar of events. These include two transfer fairs, with an average attendance of approximately 500 students and over 100 four-year college transfer personnel. The office also assists with managing the institution's multiple articulation agreements and communicating the specifics of each agreement campus-wide. In addition to hosting college and university personnel at the Westchester Community College Campus throughout the year in on-site admissions events, the office also coordinates transfer visits to nearby campuses. Their transfer promotion portfolio also includes classroom presentations and trainings on the use of CollegeFish.org, as well as individualized one-on-one transfer counseling and preparation sessions with students.

LESSONS LEARNED

Continuous, collaborative, campus-wide, and consistent messaging of transfer best practices is the heart of successful community college transfer support. Engagement must begin early to maximize effectiveness and to position students to avoid the transfer traps of taking excess credits, leaving unmet prerequisites, and creating unmet financial support due to the cost of transfer. Driving all transfer plans and programming should be the leveraging of opportunities to educate all community college transfer stakeholders–students, staff, faculty, and administrators–inside and outside of the classroom, while integrating on and off-campus resources.

RECOMMENDATIONS AND LIMITATIONS

Staffing, resource and budget allocation, and time are areas of concern for all public community colleges. The scope of responsibilities for community college personnel continues to expand and has intensified due to the increasing public scrutiny on community college completion and transfer success rates. Performance-based funding formulas, national rankings of colleges, and increasing interest in tuition-free community college, on both state and national levels, are major considerations for community colleges as they seek to prepare, refine, and revise transfer programming in ways that most effectively promote student completion and transfer.

COST OF THE INITIATIVE AND SOURCE OF FUNDING

Based on the components included in the community college transfer programming plan and desired outcomes, cost will vary. By sharing responsibilities and merging resources and staff, community colleges can most effectively and efficiently maximize their opportunities for success in supporting early transfer engagement. One should explore and research grant opportunities as well as seek support from university partners and statewide organizations.

References

Shapiro, D., Dundar, A., Wakhungu, P.K, Yuan, X., & Harrell, A. (2015, July). *Transfer and Mobility: A National View of Student Movement in Postsecondary Institutions, Fall 2008 Cohort* (Signature Report No. 9). Herndon, VA: National Student Clearinghouse Research Center.

Handel, S. (2013). *Recurring Trends and Persistent Themes: A Brief History of Transfer*. Retrieved from http://media.collegeboard.com/digitalServices/pdf/advocacy/policycenter/recurring-trends-persistent-themes-history-transfer-brief.pdf.

Noel-Levitz. (2013). *2013 Noel-Levitx Research Report: The Attitudes and Motivations of College Transfer Students*. Retrieved from https://www.ruffalonl.com/upload/Papers_and_Research/2013/2013TransferStudentAttitudesReport.pdf.

CCSSE's Center for Community College Student Engagement. (2012). *A Matter of Degrees: Promising Practices for Community College Student Success (A First Look)*. Austin, TX: The University of Texas at Austin, Community College Leadership Program.

Institutional Description

Name and Location:
Westchester Community College, located in Valhalla, New York

Institution Type:
Public two-year community college—part of the State University System of New York

Institutional Selectivity:
Open access

Size of Enrollment:
~13,000 students

Jennifer L. Blalock *is the chief student support officer at Phi Theta Kappa.*

Robin Graff *is the coordinator of transfer services and Phi Theta Kappa advisor at Westchester Community College, State University of New York (SUNY).*

14

Why Private Institutions May Be a Good Transfer Option for Students and Advisors to Consider

Beth Zielinski and Nancy Sanchez

Statement of the Issue

Most discussions about transfer focus on improving transfer to four-year public institutions. And with good reason, as public institutions not only have more capacity than private institutions but a mission to educate the public. Yet, private institutions are an option, and in some cases, a better option for many community college students.

Short Overview

For students whose only college exposure was to larger, public, urban commuter campuses, a small private liberal arts college or research university offers an entirely different, and sometimes challenging, experience compared with transferring to a public institution. Challenges range from identifying, applying to, and selecting a college to credit transfer to the transition itself. Whether it's a matter of increased resources and opportunities available to students, or being in a majority traditional-aged environment where many students pay full tuition and come from college-going backgrounds, the transition is significant. However, there are things that can be done to prepare and support students for the transition pre-transfer as well as once they are on the transfer institution's campus.

Program Overview

The Jack Kent Cooke Foundation, founded in 2000 as a private independent foundation based in Northern Virginia, has awarded $130 million in scholarships to 1,900 students along with more than $80 million in grants to organizations that support its mission. Its endowment has grown to more than $700 million. The Cooke Foundation's scholarship programs are designed to encourage and support high-achieving students with financial need. The Cooke scholarships provide financial assistance and academic support to high school, undergraduate, and graduate students.

The Cooke Undergraduate Transfer Scholarship makes it possible for the nation's top community college students to complete their bachelor's degrees by transferring to a four-year college or university. Applicants must be a current student at an accredited U.S. community college or two-year institution with sophomore status or a recent graduate, have a cumulative undergraduate grade point average of 3.5 or better on a scale of 4.0 (or the equivalent), and demonstrate significant unmet financial need. The Cooke Foundation provides up to $40,000 per year to each of approximately ninety deserving students selected annually, making it the largest private scholarship for two-year and community college transfer students in the country.

In addition to the financial support offered by the Cooke Undergraduate Transfer Scholarship, scholars are offered academic advising and support prior to and during their transition to the four-year institution through graduation. Scholars work with an educational adviser to first select the four-year college or university that best fits their needs. Starting with the summer before transfer, Cooke Scholars take part in a series of webinars designed to educate them on the transfer process. The scholars participate in a conference that provides programming around what to expect during the transfer transition, how to seek out and best use campus resources, how to set realistic expectations for your first semester, and how to use the Cooke Foundation support network.

Throughout their time at the four-year institution, Cooke Scholars are provided with both one-on-one and group advising around time management and study techniques, the importance of internships and research and how to seek out those opportunities, and the value of study abroad. For students facing difficulty, the educational adviser works with the scholar to create an individualized plan for academic recovery that utilizes campus resources and addresses the unique concerns of the scholar. Cooke Scholars are provided with guidance on the process to select and apply to graduate school and how to network and market themselves to either graduate schools or in the workplace. All of this advising is tailored to the transfer population, taking into account their specific needs.

The Kaplan Educational Foundation (KEF), a 501(c)(3) public charity, was initially established by a generous endowment funded by Kaplan Inc. executives. In 2006, the Kaplan Educational Foundation launched the Kaplan Leadership Program (KLP). It is a highly comprehensive program designed to provide financial aid, academic support, leadership skills development, and cultural enrichment to high-potential community colleges students beginning in the second year of their associate's degree program through completion of their bachelor's degree. The program's unique and trailblazing model is proving to fill a gap in support services within an often overlooked population of students: low-income, high-potential, historically underrepresented community college students.

KLP requires all Scholars to work one-on-one with an academic advisor and leadership coach to develop leadership at their community colleges and beyond. Scholars also work individually with a transfer admissions advisor to research and select potential transfer colleges. College lists focus on four-year programs that fit the strengths and areas of development of each Scholar. KEF's partnerships with private and public, selective four-year institutions around the nation serve to provide resources for Scholars to assess transfer institutions through direct communication with geographically-designated admissions advisors, transfer admissions representatives, and financial aid advisors. These contacts provide the financial and academic advisement Scholars need to gain admissions, secure competitive financial aid packages, and most importantly - complete their undergraduate educations.

Kaplan Leadership Program Scholars also receive leadership training delivered through workshops and discussion groups given by industry leaders and other professionals. While completing their associate's degrees, Scholars also receive tutoring in college-level English, Math, and Sciences in preparation for rigorous enrollment and continuous credit attainment. Throughout their participation in our program, Scholars work together as a Cohort and are encouraged to build strong bonds with the expectation that they will serve as each other's support system. Peer support and alumni mentorship has proven to be highly effective as an added resource as Scholars navigate college selection, explore majors, and manage college life.

Students are recruited from New York and New Jersey area community colleges through strong partnerships with faculty, staff, and administrators. To qualify for KLP, applicants must have a desire to become leaders in their communities and professions and be committed to transferring to a bachelor's program immediately upon completion of an associate's degree. Applicants must meet a minimum GPA of 3.5 (on a 4.0 scale) and have completed twenty-four to thirty non-remedial credits by the end of the spring semester. Applicants must also qualify for federal and/or state financial aid, be Black/African American, Hispanic/Latino or Native American, and be U.S. Citizen or Permanent Resident.

KEF's support services begin in the second year of associate's degree studies and continue through the completion of a bachelor's degree. Financial assistance includes scholarships and additional funding to assist with other educational and living expenses, including study abroad. All KLP Scholars are provided with academic advising, transfer admissions, career counseling and job placement support, and admissions guidance for graduate and professional programs. KLP's curriculum was developed to target the academic, financial, and personal/social development of its participants reflecting the belief that the whole student must be addressed to affect long-term success. There are currently eight Cohorts of KLP Scholars, including twenty active KLP Scholars in the program and twenty-five alumni. KEF is currently selecting their ninth cohort. KLP Scholars are attending highly competitive four-year schools while program Alumni have graduated with honors, landing notable positions in their fields of interest and earning degrees from highly selective graduate schools.

End Result and Impact

Nearly half of Cooke Undergraduate Transfer Scholars attend private institutions. Cooke Scholars, most of whom are first generation college students, have a ninety-seven percent completion rate, in three years or less. Since its inception in 2006, 100 percent of Kaplan Leadership Program Scholars transferring from the City University of New York's system have enrolled in a private four-year college or university. Over ninety percent—all of whom are low-income as well as Black or Hispanic—earn a bachelor's degree within two to three years of completing an associate's degree. Cooke and Kaplan Scholars are attending private institutions including Amherst, Brown, Columbia, Georgetown, New York University, Stanford, and Yale. The completion timing of both program's scholars suggest that the private institutions are accepting credits and providing the support needed to students coming from community colleges.

Nationally, less than one out of 1,000 students at a selective private institution are community college transfers (Dowd et al., 2006). These numbers suggest an under matching of high-achieving community college students with private institutions. Fifty-six percent of Cooke Undergraduate Transfer Scholars graduate from highly selective colleges. Advising and support programs, such as those offered by Cooke and Kaplan, are assisting high-achieving community college students to attend and succeed at better-matched institutions.

Achievement of Cooke Scholars continues beyond the initial transfer. Forty-seven percent of Cooke Undergraduate Transfer Scholars enrolled in graduate school, compared with nineteen percent of students who applied for (but did not receive) the Cooke Scholarship (Giancola, 2014). Once again, the tailored-to-the-transfer advising provided by the Foundation may have a significant impact for career preparation and post-graduation success.

Recommendations and Limitations

Private selective institutions must be presented as an option to community college students contemplating transfer admissions and the necessary information and resources should be made available for students to apply to these institutions.

Low-income, first-generation community college students can successfully transfer and thrive at selective senior colleges and universities and remain academically competitive.

Academic advisement in contemplation of transfer must consider the strengths and areas of development of high potential students in order to identify the community college resources needed to address both, and prepare the student to succeed at any four-year institution.

Consistent and continuous academic advisement until completion of four-year degree from the host program (Cooke, KLP) plays a significant role in addressing road blocks, navigating, and fully taking advantage of resources at transfer colleges.

Many selective four-year institutions throughout the nation have the resources to admit and properly support the goals of high-achieving and high-potential community college transfer students. However, it is importantly to properly assess each institution's transfer resources and their commitment to their transfer community. It is important to encourage four-year institutions to address the unique needs of transfer students.

The financial support (scholarships) has been integral in demonstrating affordability of private four-year institutions. However, with many schools seeking to meet 100 percent of need, we have seen that a community college student can have multiple acceptances with minimal to no student or family contribution.

Providing a living stipend has been a vital tool to enable students to engage more fully in their studies and extracurricular activities to prepare them for future leadership roles.

REFERENCES

Dowd, A., Bensimon, E.M., Gabbard, G., Singleton, S., Macias, E., Dee, J.,… & Giles, D. (2006) *Threading the needle of the American dream, executive summary.*

Giancola, J. (2014) *Analysis of post-applicant outcomes of cooke scholarship applicants.*

Unpublished analysis of data obtained from the National Student Clearinghouse.

Beth Zielinski *is a senior educational advisor at the Jack Kent Cooke Foundation.*

Nancy Sanchez *the executive director of the Kaplan Educational Foundation.*

EPILOGUE

Eileen Strempel

The articles presented in this volume represent the collective work of practitioners throughout the United States who are devoted to the academic success of community college students seeking baccalaureate degrees. Each contribution emphasizes that community colleges comprise the most popular postsecondary education sector in America today, providing low-cost access and educational opportunity for students at a fraction of the cost associated with four-year public and private universities.

The recent increased focus on transfer students manifests itself in extraordinary ways, ranging from the President of the United States establishing aspirational educational goals, to the rising interest of state policy makers in community colleges as essential for affordable college completion. Our recovery from the Great Recession has instilled important lessons, one of which is the greater value American families place on the cost of a college degree. Although community colleges can and do provide a more affordable avenue to the baccalaureate, the transfer process has remained convoluted, complicated, and complex. Our most vulnerable students begin their postsecondary education at a community college, yet these students are often the least equipped to navigate the frequently choppy waters of transfer in the middle of their undergraduate career.

Furthermore, the current process makes vast assumptions. For example, students are frequently required to carefully select courses during their first semester at a community college to avoid losing course credit when they transfer. This is despite the fact that most students don't yet know which degree path they will ultimately select. When community college students do manage to transfer, the receiving institution may or may not have a transfer-receptive culture. Ironically, even though many four-year institutions highly value the tuition revenue transfer students provide to institutional coffers, transfer students are not always welcomed more broadly. Faculty, staff and student colleagues may stereotype transfer students as less talented, less meritorious, and less qualified than "traditional" students. Transfer students are all too frequently left to fend for themselves outside of the supportive environment of student housing. In addition, transfer students frequently find themselves locked out of honors or study abroad programs, unable to traverse the byzantine faculty gauntlet essential to developing the deep connections and research opportunities required for more elite graduate programs or the best job opportunities.

Our inability to accommodate the needs of transfer students is an educational travesty—as the research from this volume documents. For example, it is estimated that two-thirds of community college students have a household income below $50,000 a year (including their parents' income if they are dependents), and the household income of half of these students is below $30,000 (Radwin, Wine, Siegel, Bryan, & Hunt-White, 2013). This means two-thirds of our nation's community college students are eligible for the Pell Grant. An effective community college transfer process has the potential to be a powerful catalyst for individual economic mobility and heightened lifetime earnings for low-income students.

Fortunately, this collection of best practices begins to capture the innovative work of practitioners across the country engaged in creating sustained and strategic partnerships dedicated to the success of our nation's transfer students. This volume captures the insights gleaned from years of experience by transfer champions from across the country. We hope that it will speak to all of us seeking new ideas about how to provide the best access and support to our transfer students.

The three broad categories of this book address some of the most pressing issues by focusing on key aspects of the transfer process: strategic planning, curricular innovations and initiatives, and outreach and advising. Many of the articles recognize that transfer is a shifting landscape, and the most imaginative promising practices now emphasize deep collaboration, and shared implementation over the long-term. All of the practices shared evoke a general movement away from transactional gestures towards the building of genuine relational connections with transfer students.

One of the most disputed and protected arenas in the transfer discussion remains the curricula. Curricula are most frequently designed with the "traditional" student in mind, and are generally owned by the faculty as the caretakers of a particular institution's identity and academic ethos. Thus, the intentional development of transfer learning communities is a welcome bridge-building strategy for fostering important connections across the campus community, weaving the faculty and the institution's curriculum into a substantive web of support. The creation of targeted learning communities for specific majors such as engineering or for students with veteran status leverages a cohort concept, with a focus on supporting and nurturing transfer students sharing a common academic interest or background. The potential for deepening transfer-affirming institutional cultures using cohort models is vast and deserves deeper exploration and expansion.

Outreach and advising have long been recognized as vital to the transfer process, due to the inherently complex nature of moving across institutional boundaries. Some of the most promising practices attempt to ameliorate these challenges by co-locating two-year and four-year services at the community college. The collaborative work of the Jack Kent Cooke Foundation and the Kaplan Educational Foundation present an inspired model. These foundations adopt a transfer student ethos that abandons the single gesture of *transfer* (evoking the wire transferring of funds), and moves towards a longitudinal and personal *transitional* advising and mentoring framework that transcends institutional boundaries. Many of the included articles reinforce this focus on providing proactive, consistent advising and support to community college students as they navigate their collegiate pathway.

Whether developing and implementing a strategic plan designed to foster an institutional transfer-receptive culture, or by working at the state level (as exemplified by Minnesota and New York), practitioners are addressing persistent complaints about transfer as they create policies and programs designed to enhance the transfer process. Yet, significant limitations remain for students transferring outside of a particular institution's welcoming ecosystem or for those students transitioning from public community colleges to private four-year institutions.

WICHE's Interstate Passport Initiative with its "transportable" curriculum is revolutionary, because it crosses state lines. While this effort is encouraging, it points to the need for broader, national efforts, like a national transfer pathway partnership. In a recent report, The Edvance Foundation (Edvance Foundation, 2015) presents a promising model including virtual bridge programs and the creation of a network of mentors for community college students staffed in regional offices and funded by four-year institutional membership fees and corporate sponsors. Whatever our response, unless we articulate a more comprehensive solution, we will miss the opportunity to realize transfer's full potential to combat our nation's economic inequality at scale.

The challenge for higher education in America is to provide access to all talented students, regardless of their socio-economic status. Fixing the transfer process is absolutely essential. There is too much at stake, for our students and our country. As a nation, if we recruit, admit, enroll, and support more community college students, ensuring their successful transfer and baccalaureate degree completion, we will positively impact the growing economic disparity in our country. The inspiring efforts of committed transfer practitioners challenge our policy makers to match these promising practices with a coordinated, national response to foster our future workforce and citizens.

REFERENCES

Radwin, D., Wine, J. Siegel, P., Bryan, M., & Hunt-White, T. (2013, August). *2011–12 National Postsecondary Student Aid Study (NPSAS:12)*. Retrieved from http://nces.ed.gov/pubs2013/2013165.pdf

Edvance Foundation. (2015, November). *Strengthening the Transfer Pathway from Community to Private Colleges*. Retrieved from http://edvancefoundation.org/transfer-report/